Meet Me in the Treehouse

Kelly Tink

Middlemist Publishing

To everyone who believed in
and supported me.
This is for you.

Prologue

Chris is quicker than me and I'm out of breath by the time we reach the treehouse ladder. He scoots up first, but I wish he'd let me. I almost trip, trying to go faster than my feet can move, scared of the trees and their shadows behind us.

"Did you bring the torches?" I ask, bobbing my head as my eyes search the four wooden walls and pointy roof.

"It's not even dark yet, don't be such a chicken, Em."

"I'm not a chicken, I just don't like the dark." I hear him laugh and I frown. It was his idea to camp out here. Well, a little bit my idea, but mostly his.

"It'll be fun," he says.

"Did you bring the snacks?" I ask, before he starts calling me a scaredy cat, which I am, but I hate it all the same.

He unzips his rucksack, removing a bottle of dandelion and burdock, before turning it upside down—shaking out rustling packets that fall into a heap by our knees with a thud.

"Bagsy the bacon flavour Wheat Crunchies," I say, diving my hand into the pile to grab a pack. He shakes his head, but I know he bought these for me.

I'm not sure how long we've been out, but it's dark now. Chris turned on the torch without me asking, and is now busy picking out cola bottles from his white paper sweet bag, shoving them into his mouth.

"Do you think your parents bought that you're sleeping at mine?"

"I think so, yours?"

"Yeh. Stephen's covering for me anyway."

"Cool."

Chris sucks in his stomach, puffs out his chest, and lets out a burn-your-nose burp, then laughs.

"Gross!"

"You're welcome!"

My legs start to judder and he throws me a blanket. I didn't think it would be so cold in the treehouse. We're only normally here in the day, when the sun's on it. I wrap the soft brown fleecy material around my shoulders and tuck it under my knees.

"I feel a bit sick," I say.

"I told you not to eat all that sherbet."

I hear a bump on the roof, and twist round. "What's that?"

"Scaredy cat!"

"You jumped too."

"Only coz you did. It was just a twig, or something, but if you're that worried you can sit with me, if you like."

I bum-shuffle over to him and lean against the treehouse wall as he slides closer, wafting his blanket over my legs. I'm warmer now, next to him, and I don't feel scared anymore, though he's still shining the torch with its bright white light on the closed door.

"Just a twig," I whisper. He doesn't say anything back, but I see him put the torch on the floor. "You still gutted Stephen didn't come with us?"

"No," he says with a huff. "You? For Lucy, I mean."

"No. I know she's not into camping."

"My sister's too much of a princess and my brother is too *in love*," he says, wrapping his arms around his body, making kissing sounds. We both giggle. "Least there's always you and me," he says, looking straight ahead.

"You and me forever," I say, holding my little finger in the air.

"What?"

"Pinky promise …" I stare at him, my best dimples on show.

He wraps his little finger around mine. "Don't tell anyone I did this," he says, and I let out the loudest burp of my life.

"Urgh, gross!"

"I won't tell if you won't."

We both roll over laughing.

Chapter 1

Twenty-one years later ...

"Hi," Chris says, standing in the doorway of my parents' living room, tilting his head to one side.

"I wish people wouldn't do that!" I reply.

"What?"

I imitate the gesture.

"Oh, the sympathetic head tilt. Did I?"

I nod. "It's irritating." When I notice my best friend's shoulders sink, I immediately feel guilty for sounding so harsh.

Untangling myself from the pile of blankets I'm encased in, I stand up, pulling the hem of my jumper down firmly over my skin-tight leggings. I see him catch sight of me and try to ignore the weight of his stare as I set about straightening the blankets and pillows on the sofa. Anything to delay having to look at him. When I finally turn around, the warmth in his eyes makes my bottom lip tremble and an unwilling tear falls from my eye. Then, in an instant, I'm in his arms.

"I'm sorry," I say, my body shuddering against his.

"You don't have anything to be sorry for," he whispers, his voice comforting me more than his words do. As does his chin resting on top of my head.

"Do you want to talk about it?" he asks, taking a seat on the sofa, drawing me beside him.

"I'm not sure I even know where to start." I hear the muffled words leave my lips, my clenched fist too tight against them to let the words flow unhindered.

"We were arguing." I cast him a knowing sideways glance. "Even more than normal." I return my stare to the fixed position on the carpet that had my prior attention. "He began working late all the time and when he was at home he was distant." My pace quickens. "He told me he wasn't smoking again, but his breath smelt of cigarettes, so I knew he was lying." I sigh. "One of many it seems …" He only ever smoked when he was unhappy, so I should have known it was bad. I just wasn't expecting he would …" I shake my head and squeeze my eyes shut.

Chris's hand finds my own.

"It's this feeling of shock that's so hard to shake." Once more my body trembles involuntarily and I release the backed-up tears from my eyes, making everything as blurry in my sight as it is in my mind. Then I'm pulled back into his arms where he holds me in silence.

I feel more in control now as the warm jets of a much-needed shower hit my skin and awaken me for what feels like the first time this week. Chris has insisted I eat something and there is no point in arguing with him, but to be honest I feel sick at the idea of leaving the house. Another thing he insists will '*do me good*'. I've not seen anyone, aside from my parents, having been screening Chris and Lucy's calls for days. Unsurprising that he turned up unannounced, though I would have expected Lucy to be with him.

I've somewhat dwelled on my misfortune since arriving home at my parents' just over a week ago, after being unceremoniously kicked out of my home. I couldn't face anyone, or more particularly, their sympathy. However, if I'm being truthful, I mostly can't face their '*I told you sos*'. I don't believe any of my friends would be so overtly uncaring as to say this to my face. Thinking it, however, is a different matter—and perhaps this wouldn't be uncaring, it would simply be the truth.

By the time we leave I do feel hungry and decide to leave it up to him to choose where to go, though I hope he knows I'm not ready to face any of the villagers. The rumour mill will be rife, which is no surprise in a small, rural Derbyshire village such as Pineham. Everyone knows everyone, and his or her business. Chris knows me well enough to know I'm not strong enough to face that at the moment.

Half an hour later, it's confirmed how well he knows me as we pull into the car park of The Duck Pond. Deep in the country, with its unassuming whitewashed walls, gravel car park, and single blackboard outside announcing 'Today's Specials', the pub is renowned for its great food and, happily for me, has many tables in nooks that are perfect for hiding out of sight. It was also one of our old favourite places.

Stepping out of the car my warm breath meets with cold air and swirls in front of my face. Winter is my favourite season. Every year I hope for snow just like when we were kids, spending hours sledging and building igloos—back in the days when a snow day was just that, not a light dusting, gone by lunchtime. We were practically blue when our parents dragged us inside. My mum would make us hot chocolate sprinkled with marshmallows and we'd toast the remaining marshmallows on sticks over the open fire. All of a sudden, I long for those days and their simplicity.

I pull my thick brown cardigan around my ears to shield myself from the cold as I follow him towards the pub's entrance.

"How about over there?" he asks, pointing to the furthest away table, by the fire.

I nod.

The inside of the pub is quaint and quirky in equal measure. The beamed ceilings are low, much like those back at my parents' farmhouse, and the shelves lined with brass tankards, horseshoes, and pottery.

"I'll get the drinks. What would you like?" he asks.

"A glass of prosecco, please."

Over at the bar he steals a look back in my direction. I think right about now he's wishing he'd invited Lucy along. After all, frequenting the local pub and drinking prosecco was my and Lucy's thing. It had become somewhat a tradition for the two of us to order a bottle and chat about our respective worlds. We hadn't even broken with tradition in the past five years while I was living in Kent. Chris had once been party to this tradition, although not in recent years.

"The barman's bringing the drinks over," he says, as he returns to the table, draping his jacket over the chair opposite me. A familiar picture of a windmill hangs behind him on a pale blue wall. Several other pictures and paintings dotted around the room are of local landmarks, such as churches, castles, picturesque beauty spots, and country estates. A painting of Wincastle, Chris's family estate, features in the collection.

"Is that the painting your parents gave to the previous owners?"

"Yes." He gives it a fleeting glance.

"I haven't been here as often since the new people took over. It's nice they haven't felt the need to change much. The food is just as good too."

"Always thinking of food, eh, Christopher! Some things don't change."

"That's better."

"What?"

"You sound like you, that's all."

"I'm sorry."

"Stop apologising."

I dip my head to acknowledge his point. “Why’s Lucy not here? Is she mad that I’ve been avoiding you both this past week?”

“Why would she be mad? We’re just worried about you.”

“I.” A long-drawn-out sigh leaves me. “I couldn’t face you both.”

His hand touches mine just as the waiter approaches with our drinks.

“I’m pretty sure I said a glass, not a bottle? Am I drinking this by myself, Christopher?” I tip the bottleneck forward in the ice bucket, making a crunching sound.

“I’m driving, so I’m only having a beer, and it makes more sense to order a bottle than pay by the glass.”

I wait for a second.

“Okay, so, I think you need to get really drunk and forget the loser for one night. There, I said it.”

I can’t help but smile. “Okay. Cheers.” I raise my glass to his pint. “To forgetting the loser.”

“I’ll drink to that. Cheers.” He clinks with enthusiasm.

The fire cracks and pops as the logs burn down into ashes behind us. Basking in its warmth, I circle my finger around the champagne flute, feeling as though I’m ever so slightly moving in slow motion.

"Did you stop coming here after Stephen died?" I ask, my tone elevated.

Chris's older brother Stephen died in a car accident when he was just twenty-six years old. Chris had been twenty-four at the time and it had been tough on everyone, not least his parents.

"Yes," he admits flatly.

I watch his Adam's apple rise and fall as he swallows.

"It was too hard to come back at first." His shoulders sag. "I can't believe it's been eight years since we lost him. Sometimes it feels like it was only yesterday and sometimes it feels longer, you know?" He pauses. "Anyway, we're here for you to talk, not me."

I consider pressing him on the subject, but he's clearly trying to divert the conversation back to me, or at least away from Stephen.

"Tell me about you," I say. "What's new in life? It's been a while since we had the chance to do this." I'm also trying to divert the conversation away from myself.

"I can do that." He smiles. "I've officially made it to the dizzy heights of estate manager."

"Lucy said something about that. Are you enjoying it?"

He scratches his head. "Enjoying may not be the right word. It can be quite a challenge keeping up with all the events we host and businesses we run these days. Horse trials, food markets, classic car rallies, art exhibitions, weddings, business conferences, team-building days. We have more staff than ever, and I'm constantly looking at new ways to keep the board of trustees happy and make the estate more income, but at least it keeps me out of trouble."

"I hear the orangery restaurant is doing well."

"Very much so."

"I was in the farm shop with Mum last time I was home. You have quite an impressive range of cheeses."

He laughs. "Have you been in the sculpture gardens yet?"

I shake my head.

"You should. It's proving quite popular, especially since we added water features for the kids to play in. Or you could just take a picnic by the river."

"Sounds right up my street. How's Granny with all the changes?"

"As archaic as ever!" He pulls a pompous face. "Mum always says Granny would have been better suited to the Victorian era, which is odd because she was raised in the swinging sixties. She hated all my grandfather's entrepreneurial ideas, too, but it was he and his father before him that saved the estate, allowing us to still live in the family home and make a living from it. If she'd had her way, who knows where we'd all be now."

"You'd have real jobs like the rest of us." I laugh as Chris shakes his head, all too familiar with my mocking of his glamorous lifestyle, though I know it's not half as glamorous as it appears.

"Earth to Emma."

I jump, sending my glass flying in his direction.

Prosecco floods his lap and he leaps to his feet.

"I'm so sorry!"

He brushes down the front of his jeans with his hands.

"I'm such a klutz!"

"It's reassuring really."

"What is?"

"That you're still as clumsy as ever. A trait that's provided me with endless amusement over the years." He wipes his hands on a napkin and I want to wipe the smile off his cheeky face. "Care to share your distraction, given it ended in me being hosed in fizz?"

"I was just daydreaming about how things used to be."

"The good ole days."

"The good ole days."

He closes his eyes and takes a long breath. "I miss those days."

"Me too."

Chapter 2

Reluctantly, I open my eyes and try to sit up, though my head feels as if an elastic band is holding me down. Instead, I roll over to see Chris asleep beside me, fling myself forward, this time with no trouble at all, checking I'm wearing clothes. *Camisole and pants, phew.* Holding my head, I don't know what to think. It's not as though I'd never shared a bed with Chris over the course of our friendship, especially as kids. I haven't shared a bed with any man aside from my husband in the past five years. I'm technically still married, however, I'm sure that the busty brunette keeping my husband's bed warm negates the need for me to feel guilty. Everything is hazy, so I lie back down and close my eyes.

It's often first thing in the morning when I forget I'm no longer someone's wife, almost as though I have amnesia. I wake up, and ten seconds later remember my life is no longer what it once was. I readjust my eyes in unfamiliar surroundings and feel the same ache in my chest from the gaping hole in my heart that had been there the day before, and the day before that.

It's still too raw for me, rawer than I can live with most days. Only four weeks ago, I was living my life unaware of what was just around the corner. At first, time stood still and nothing made sense. The pain I'm feeling is so deep it's almost made me shut down, and nothing in the past four weeks has succeeded in numbing it. Being here with Chris is the closest I've felt to some sort of relief. Though it doesn't surprise me; he's always been the one person in the world who can make anything seem more bearable.

Divorce had never been part of the plan. It wasn't something that featured on 'the list' I made aged seventeen: pass my driving test, *tick*, qualify as a nurse, *tick*, get married, *tick*, and as an aside it read 'to the man of my dreams', *not ticked*, have children and build a home for them, *not ticked*. By far the most obscure thing on the list was to 'dance with the man of my dreams to Tchaikovsky's Waltz of the Flowers', *unlikely to be ticked*. Yes, all very specific and cheesy. Perhaps heavily influenced by the fact I was a complete and utter hopeless romantic. Growing up around Wincastle only fed into that part of me. It had been like living on my very own set of *Pride and Prejudice*, what with the grandeur of the house, the grounds, the balls, and the dancing. It had felt like such a charmed life growing up. Nevertheless, it wasn't real life, not mine anyway. Almost divorced at the age of thirty, with no children and an ever-ticking clock. Living back with my parents, jobless, and having had my heart broken so badly that it seemed as though it would never repair itself, they were definitely not on the list.

Dangling my legs over the side of the bed, the coolness of the room hits me. My clothes are on the floor beneath my feet, so I dress in haste. The room begins spinning as I walk into the bathroom, where I check my appearance in the mirror. Splashing warm water on my wishy-washy face, I'm grateful not to have worn make-up, which saved me having panda eyes this morning. My general lack of self-care and the cold weather are responsible for my chapped lips. There's a foul taste of alcohol lingering on my tongue and my mouth is dry, making me wish I could brush my teeth. Instead, I settle for swilling my mouth with tap water.

Running my fingers through my hair from root to tip, it feels wiry and unconditioned and its depth of colour only adds to my pallor. Pausing, I stare at my reflection—*this is as good as it gets right now.* Chris has seen me in worse states, and then I take one last look in the mirror and reconsider: perhaps not. Not that it matters, he's my best friend, or at least he was.

Chris is still out cold when I re-enter the room. Rummaging through my handbag, I pull out a small hairbrush and lip balm. Standing in front of the full-length mirror behind the door, I scrape my long chestnut strands into a tight ponytail and apply a generous amount of balm to my lips. I look back at Chris and notice his skin has an unseasonable tan and that the dark blond hair resting over his forehead is a shade lighter, perhaps from recent travel. Not that I've asked him, or did I? I have no recollection of anything from the night before. I've been drunk before, but never with quite the same effect. Maybe it's due to the fact that my appetite has all but disappeared recently, which in turn means my weight is at the lowest it's been in adult years. Where I used to be a healthy ten and a half stone, I'm now nearer to eight and my doctor has said that my hip bones should not protrude the way they do. It was more the look of worry on the doctor's face that concerned me most. I look anorexic, this I know. Not more so than when I stand in front of the mirror naked and I can see for myself what others only see through my clothes, my bones. It's unhealthy, yet there seems to be nothing I can do to control it. My emotions dictate my appetite and my appetite dictates my weight. The doctor called it 'acute anxiety', and recommended time off work and some counselling. I pull my cardigan around my body, uncomfortable at the thought Chris would have seen the way I look last night. I hate my body the way it is.

The frosty morning sky, mixed with the bright winter sunshine, is streaming into the room through the voile curtains. As I draw them aside, I squint, adjusting my eyes to look out at the perfect view of the rolling countryside. There are green undulating hills for miles that appear to form the tops of love hearts in rows. It's comforting being in the middle of nowhere. I contemplate, and not for the first time, running away. Though I conclude, as I have so many times in the past four weeks, running away is not the answer. Even if I wish I could be miles away from anyone. It's a beautiful wintry day, and if nothing else, I don't feel quite so alone anymore. Not here with Chris.

Feeling thirsty and wishing to rid my mouth of its foul taste, I fill the small kettle with water from the bathroom sink. Chris stirs to the sound of it boiling and strains to open his eyes in the patch of sunlight resting on his face.

"Sorry." I cross the room to shut the curtains. "Is that better?"

"Thanks," Chris croaks. He clears his throat with a cough before sitting up onto his elbows, arm muscles flexed and balancing his weight. I almost blush as I notice his well-defined curves.

"Coffee?" I hold up a mug, trying to sound casual.

Chris rubs his eyes. "Yes, please."

I hand him a steaming mug and perch on the bed beside him.

"Thank you. How rough are you on a scale of one to dying?" he asks.

"Me? I'm fine."

"I've got some painkillers in the car. I'll get dressed and get them for you," he says.

"How did you guess?"

"What, that you're hung-over or that your head's killing you?" He rolls his eyes at me. "You always get a headache when you've been drinking and you normally try and hide it. Though I don't know why. You've always been a lightweight!"

"Hey, who are you calling a lightweight?"

Chris shrugs, smiling.

"So, what's *your* excuse for the hangover that I know you have?" I'm trying to sound more offended than I am, because I know just how little drink I can handle, especially in comparison to him. Some things don't change between us.

"I hadn't anticipated you wanting to drink so much, so I joined in with the prosecco in an attempt to slow you down. Then we both got drunk, and if I remember correctly, we did a shot or three … I'm not sure how many in the end."

"Shots!" I slap my forehead. "I warned you years ago to never let me do shots, ever again."

He's laughing. "I'd forgotten just how highly amusing you are when you're drunk, by the way."

This time I roll my eyes at him. "How do you even remember stuff about last night?"

"Because I, unlike you, can handle my drink."

I try to play punch his arm, but he dodges my fist and climbs out of bed.

"You okay?" he asks me, pulling on his jeans, "you look a bit green, Em."

I wince, thrusting my mug at him, and make a run for the bathroom.

"Do you need me to hold back your hair?" he jokes after me, in reference to the time when he did, actually, have to hold back my hair as I vomited on one of our teenage nights out.

"I hate you!" I lie gingerly back down beside him on the bed when I return.

"Me? Hey what did I do?"

"You got me drunk."

"You got you drunk. I distinctly remember telling you to slow down, *lightweight*." He coughs out the last word behind his clenched fist.

I don't have the energy to scowl at him.

I close my eyes as the room is still spinning and I don't know when it will stop. I fear having to stand, or worse still, eat something. Both of which are imminent if Chris has anything to do with it.

"Here, drink this." Chris offers me a cup of water and I sit up. "Do you still need those painkillers?" he asks.

I shake my head tentatively. Swallowing anything more than this sip of water right now would prove difficult, and likely result in more sprints to the bathroom.

"Hmmm, right, miss, breakfast time."

I grimace and flop back on the pillow.

"Resistance is futile," he says in a most confused accent. For which I would mock him if I felt better, but I don't.

Chris has an understated sense of humour. I can think of countless times over the years at estate dinner parties when he would lean over to whisper something funny in my ear, just for my benefit. His quiet wit was always so well placed that I couldn't help but laugh when he was poking fun at his uptight grandmother or another hoity-toity guest that we'd been forced to endure an evening with. He would always say that making me laugh was the least he could do for agreeing to accompany him to 'these things'.

I remember he would beg me to change my plans and be his guest to dinners and balls. I would of course protest, not because I minded, more that it amused me having him grovel. Truth is, I used to love those evenings more than he did and I relished every opportunity to attend. I also wanted to be there to support him. Stephen had been the natural future heir, primed from a young age to inherit the estate and title from their father. In many ways, because of this, Chris had been overlooked, something which he never minded. I always felt that he wished he could have a normal life, instead of the one he'd been born into.

In no time, we're making our way back across the car park to the pub for breakfast. He opens the door ahead of me and the waiter seats us. Chris's hangover cure is food. In fact, I believe it's his cure for most things, and despite how little food appeals right now, it's always worked for me in the past.

"What can I get you, madam?" the waiter asks.

"Some toast, please." I gulp back the urge to vomit again at the thought of anything else.

"Certainly. And for you, sir?"

"Full English and two teas, please?" Chris looks at me for approval and I nod in agreement.

"I can't believe you can face a breakfast and that you're going to make me watch you eat it. Well, I can believe it actually."

"You could always switch tables." Chris gestures to a vacant table next to us. "Besides, breakfast is their best meal here, and how do you expect to absorb all that alcohol if you just eat a bit of toast?"

"Oh, did you forget that my stomach contents departed from me about half an hour ago?"

"Yeah, how could I forget that?" He grimaces.

I sit back, my arms folded, but my dimples give me away.

"It's nice to see you smiling." He sits back also.

"It's nice to have someone to smile with."

I reflect that it is nice to have someone to smile with, though it feels strange. Good strange I think, although strange nonetheless. I didn't expect to enjoy myself and smile so much when Chris suggested leaving the house yesterday. In fact, in many ways it feels wrong. I feel guilty even, given my situation. No one has died, though some days it feels as though they have. I feel as if I'm in mourning. Mourning the loss of the life I've built and known for the past five years and the future I thought would be mine. Then in an instant, it's gone. It plagues me every day that I didn't see it coming.

Perhaps it's part of some inbuilt defence mechanism to ignore, or at least refuse to face up to what was really happening in my marriage. Marriage is tough, tougher than I'd realised it would be as a starry-eyed twenty-something-year-old. Being innately traditional, something Chris and I share, we believe in marriage for life, like our parents and grandparents. Not finding out the hard way that love isn't all you imagined it to be.

"Emma?"

I turn to my left and see a familiar face standing beside our table.

"Jo!" I push back my seat, standing to hug her. "What are you doing here?"

"I'm meeting my mum for breakfast … How are you?"

I tilt my head from side to side. "I've been better."

"I'm so sorry. I bumped into your mum the other day and she said you were home, but that you weren't feeling up to seeing people."

"She did tell me actually. Sorry, my mind is all over the place."

"Of course. Don't apologise. I'm here, though, if you want to go for a drink. Just message me on Facebook, or something?"

"I will. Sorry, this is Chris, my old friend. I don't know if you guys ever met?"

"Hi Chris, we did a couple of times, I think."

"Hi Jo, yes. It was at Emma's twenty-first birthday party, and then a BBQ at her parents', right?"

"Wow, you have an exceptional memory."

"Thanks." He smiles.

"Anyway." Jo draws me in for another hug and this time squeezes me more tightly. "You take care, and message me, okay?"

"I will, promise." I let go of her and smile.

"You guys trained as nurses together, didn't you?" Chris asks after Jo leaves us.

"Yes. We met on day one at uni and we were inseparable after that. We've been through a lot together over the years."

"Then you should call her, arrange to catch up. You never know, she might know of a job for you."

After breakfast, the journey home passes in peaceful silence as I look out over the fields and valleys that remind me how much I love the countryside. It's in my blood. Even the smell of manure conjures up fond memories, as opposed to disgust. It's been a normal smell growing up on a farm. My grandfather, having been a keen pig farmer, smelt of pigs most of my life. He'd even once named a baby piglet after me and, to this day, the memory makes me happy, even more in recent years since his passing. My parents still have livestock on the farm, though the numbers have dwindled over time due to all the health scares and trauma that farming has endured.

When I was about twelve years old, I went down to the farm on Easter Sunday with my dad to feed the animals. I used to check on the broody hens sitting on eggs and encourage them to come off to have some food. On that day, when I opened the hatch, I found three beautiful fluffy chicks: two yellow and one brown. I remember picking them up, cradling them in my hands. I love animals. I love that I know how to take care of them and it's more second nature to me than being a nurse.

"You seem deep in thought." Chris turns off the engine.

I hadn't realised we were back and already parked on my parents' driveway.

"Just reminiscing." I unbuckle my seat belt and slip it over my arm. "Hope I haven't been bad company?" I face him.

"You're never bad company, Em. I feel pretty helpless, that's all."

"Well, last night helped a lot, even if I can't remember a thing. In fact, it was good not to remember for a night. Perhaps I should start drinking every night."

The slight rise of his left eyebrow tells me he thinks it's a bad idea as he leans over to kiss my cheek.

I climb out of the car. "Thank you." I bob my head down to see inside.

"My pleasure."

Chapter 3

My car follows the gentle curve of the driveway that runs all the way to the east courtyard. As I near the house, an impressive skyline of octagonal turrets comes into view that sit so high they seem to pierce the low winter sunshine. The large electronic wrought-iron gates open in front of me and I drive into the old stable block. Climbing out of the car, I shield my face with my hands from the sun that isn't helping my hangover. Partially dragging my feet, I walk through the passageway into the courtyard, which sits in the shadows of the big house. In front of me stands a row of three-storey limestone terraced cottages which house long-serving members of staff. There are some newer staff quarters in the estate grounds. Beside the cottages, a stone archway leads to the east wing, the family's private residence.

Chris opens the door, tipping his head to the side.

I hold up my bags. "Mind if I stay for a few days?"

Without words or hesitation, he takes my things and moves aside.

"Barney, hey boy." Chris's black Labrador dog

bundles into me, licking my hand as I reach out to stroke him. I scruff his ears, his tail whipping side to side. "Aw, I've missed you too," I say in a voice reserved only for cute animals.

"Down boy, come on, let her past." He pats Barney on the top of his head.

We pass a picture of Stephen in the hallway, his familiar eyes smiling at me from a face frozen in time. Stephen was a barrister and both exceptionally clever and the most just person I've ever had the pleasure of knowing. He had accepted his future responsibilities as the heir, but nonetheless he wanted to experience life and make a difference while he had the time and Sir Richard had supported this decision, knowing full well that when the time came, Stephen would join the family business as one of the estate's custodians, alongside Chris and Lucy, who back then enjoyed being paid for very little input or responsibility.

It doesn't surprise me to find Lucy waiting in the hallway when we step inside. She turns to Chris. "I phoned the farm and Cath said you were both out last night. Why didn't you take me with you? I asked you over breakfast if you were going over to the farm and you said no!"

I confess, I always forget how scary Lucy is when she's mad.

"I went on the off chance Emma was feeling up for visitors." Chris stands his ground.

"I'm sorry, Luce. We didn't leave you out on purpose," I say, trying to defuse the situation.

"Where did you go? You were out all night?" She places both hands on her hips and continues her line of questioning to Chris. Lucy's long bleach blonde hair and slight frame would be less intimidating had she not perfected her scowl over the years.

"We went to The Duck Pond, got drunk, collapsed in one of the rooms for the night and then came home, Sis."

I sense Chris isn't in the mood for the third degree and, quite honestly, neither am I.

"Are you okay?" Her face softens as she turns towards me and so, it seems, judging by the relaxing of his shoulders, does Chris's mood.

"I will be."

She grabs me in a bear hug.

"Please don't be mad at him. Last night was the first time in forever I felt even a little bit of normality," I whisper into her hair.

After a brief silence, she holds me at arm's length.

"I'm not mad. I was worried. We'll get you through this, okay?" Her hands slide down my arms until our fingertips entwine.

"Okay," I say, both of our eyes full of tears that don't spill.

"You can stay with me. It'll be just like old times," Lucy says, surveying me with a poorly veiled expression of shock at my emaciated appearance.

"Thank you." I turn to Chris. "Are you sure it's okay?"

He nods. "You don't even need to ask. This has

always been like your home, too, and you can stay for as long as you like. Your parents don't mind, do they?"

"I left them a note. They won't mind. If anything, they'll expect this is where I'll be."

With that, Lucy leads me away.

That afternoon, I find myself in Chris's office, overlooking the charming view of the south gardens, which happen to be my favourite. The deep green yew tree hedges shaped into formal lines create a secret garden with an archway entrance. Inside are circular flowerbeds that stand bare, but will be full of colour come the spring. Behind, the jet of the water fountain shoots up in a perfect line before curling back on itself and, further into the distance, beside the river, stands a large old oak tree. Chris and Stephen used to swing from the low-down branches of that tree as children and land in the river, usually while I watched from the bank too scared of breaking my neck to participate.

"How's the hangover?" I ask him when he finishes on the phone.

"Well, don't tell anyone I admitted this, but it's probably the worst hangover I've had in years."

"Ha! I knew it." I point at him. "So, you retired your party-boy ways then?"

"Oh you know, I've not done much of that in a while."

"I was looking at Stephen's picture in the hallway

this morning. Even after all these years, it still feels strange without him around the house."

"Yes. It can be pretty quiet around here without him."

"Quiet, with Lucy around?" I lighten the tone.

"You're right, what am I saying?" He leans back in his office chair.

Chris doesn't like to talk about Stephen, because he blames himself for his death. Stephen had been working away in London on a high-profile case, and knowing how stressed he'd been, Chris had tried to persuade him to come home for his birthday to celebrate together as they always had. Being the older brother and the sort of person who never liked to disappoint anyone, he made the trip back to the estate, crashing his car en route, only twenty minutes from home. The inquest found no obvious cause for the crash other than a suspicion that he had fallen asleep at the wheel and died instantly. It broke Chris and I'm not sure he's ever truly pieced himself back together.

"Where's my tantalising sis anyway?" he asks.

"Probably scouring the estate for me as we speak. Her plan for this evening is movies, pampering, and death by chocolate."

"Sounds very Lucy." His features are soft and playful.

I laugh. "I've missed this." I gesture back and forth in the space between us.

"Me too." His eyes lock with mine.

"There you are!" Lucy bursts in. "You can't hog

her for a second night, Christopher."

"Wouldn't dream of it, Sis. You girls have fun," he says in mocked humour for my benefit.

Despite my love for Lucy, there are times when she can be a tad exuberant and I'm not sure my mood is on a par with hers, with or without my hangover.

At around ten-thirty I knock on Chris's apartment door. It's not long before he pulls it open, wearing the same surprised face I'd seen this morning when I turned up at the house unannounced.

"Lucy's flat out in bed and I can't sleep."

He pushes back the door to let me past and I'm greeted by a familiar cold nose nuzzling the back of my hand. I stroke Barney's silky fur back.

"Are you tired?" I ask Chris.

"No."

Perching on his sofa, with Barney at my feet, I notice his laptop is open. "Am I disturbing your work?"

"No, I was finishing up for the night." He joins me on the sofa.

Picking up the laptop, I scroll over the webpage he's been browsing. *Good job it's not X-rated.* It won't faze him that I'm being nosey, I always have been.

"Food vendors?" The pitch of my voice is higher than normal.

Chris shuffles closer and slides the laptop from my

knee onto his. He scrolls the mouse to another tab, which reveals an advert. "I'm proud to announce that Wincastle is hosting a summer film festival."

My eyes widen.

"It's taking more planning than I'd anticipated, though if it's as successful as the other places I've been in touch with, we should be able to run it yearly."

"I love this. I'm sure you'll make it a success for Wincastle too."

"Thank you."

"Do you need some help?"

"I'd love some. If you're feeling up to it, that is?"

"Are you kidding me? Hand me a pen."

"A pen?"

"Because I love to make a list, Christopher."

He does as I ask and hands me a pen from the coffee table. Feeling quite revived, I begin scribbling as Chris sits back and observes.

A glass of red wine and about an hour later, Barney's asleep on my feet, snoring, and we have a shortlist of everything we think the event needs.

"So you're thinking BBQ, salad bar, ice cream, and strawberries?" he clarifies with me, pouring more wine into my glass.

"And Pimms," I say, realising I've taken over, though sensing this is somewhat a relief to him.

"Well, we can hire a licensed bar. What else haven't we covered?"

"Possible film choices …" I smirk, my pen tip poised.

Chris rests his arms over the back of the sofa. Waiting, I'm sure, for what he knows is coming next.

"I put forward my request for, drum rolls please …"

He uses both hands on the coffee table to make a beat, rousing some curiosity from the ball of fur keeping my feet warm.

"… *The Notebook*."

"You amaze me." He fake gasps and a faint sparkle emerges in his eyes. "As a thank you for helping me, you can of course have *The Notebook*," he says.

I squeak with excitement simultaneously with the unexpected growl of my stomach, and Barney retires to his bed.

"You hungry?"

"Maybe a little."

"I can make you something."

I laugh, hard.

"I'm quite self-sufficient these days, I'll have you know."

"No doubt," I say before rolling my top and bottom lips together in an attempt to stifle my amusement. I once accused him of being spoilt, saying he'd never had to do a single load of washing, or cook a meal for himself his entire life. Which was the truth. It wasn't even his fault, he'd just grown up in such a privileged life.

"I'm going to make you pancakes," he announces, pulling me to my feet.

In the kitchen, he sets about gathering the frying

pan and ingredients as if he knows his way around perfectly. I eye him with suspicion.

Soon the air fills with wafts of a warm, lightly sweet, breadlike smell. Watching him flip a pancake in the air before catching it cleanly, I applaud, laughing. The next attempt he makes more challenging, by adding a spin before catching it in the pan once more. He makes us both one large pancake each and, from the cupboard, he takes out some Nutella for the topping. My favourite.

"*Bon appetit*," he says, handing me the plate, some cutlery, and a napkin.

"Thank you, it smells amazing."

I eat it as if I've not seen food in weeks. It's only minutes before I swirl the last bite of my pancake around my plate before placing it all in my mouth.

"Good?"

I unashamedly lick my lips. "Hands down, the best pancakes I've ever tasted." I pause. "I'm impressed! Maybe you paid attention when my dad gave you lessons all those years ago. I'll be sure to tell him," I add, smiling. "Though don't tell him I said yours were the best pancakes."

"I bet you say that to all the boys." He winks, clearing the plates and leaving me with my trip down memory lane.

"You tired yet?" he asks when he returns.

I shake my head. Everything seems so much worse at night.

"I know what we can do." He disappears, so I follow him into the lounge, curious to discover what he's come up with for our entertainment. I suspect it can't be half as entertaining as discovering Chris can cook, after all these years.

"Anyone for Scrabble?"

I chuckle. "I haven't played that for years, probably since we last played, I bet."

He opens the box, finding the score sheet headed with our names.

"Ha, see!" I drag a pillow from the sofa onto the floor and make myself comfortable. He holds out the green letter bag and I rustle my hand around inside it, selecting tiles before arranging them on the rack. It's my turn first, though my frown undoubtedly tells him the inevitable letter swap is coming. More often than not, Chris would have to rescue me to make a word, or two. I would like to win, but I've never quite managed to beat him.

"I can't go," I say.

He smiles. Even if you never saw Chris's lips, you would know he's smiling just by seeing his cool grey eyes.

I drop old letters into the bag and retrieve new ones.

"So, do you often struggle to sleep?" he asks me in a low tone, rotating a tile between his fingers.

"These days." I glance up at him.

"Have you been to the doctor for something to help?"

"I don't want medication, Chris."

"I'm not saying take anything long term, perhaps it would help that's all. You look tired." Regret shows upon his face the moment the words depart from his lips.

"Gee, thanks! Make a girl feel good by telling her she looks like crap."

"I didn't say you look like crap. I said you look tired. Because you are, due to the fact you're *not sleeping.*"

It's his turn and in a stroke of pure coincidental luck, he adds the word 'TIRED' to the board.

I scowl at him and he knows he's pushing it; then again, I suspect he wants me to retaliate, because that's what the old me would do.

"Smarty pants," is all I say, catching sight of the tail end of his cheeky grin and I go back to perusing my letters. "I can't make a word." I announce and flop on my side, resting on my elbow.

Chris leans over my body, glancing at my letters to see if he can help. "Hmmm, you really don't have much luck at this game, do you?"

"You think?"

I swap more letters and let him have another turn. He places the word 'MOTHER' onto the board and I feel a pang of sadness.

"Want to tell me what you're thinking? You seemed to relax earlier, now you've drifted into your own world again."

"Sorry, I don't want to bring anyone else down."

"You keep apologising, even though you don't

have anything to apologise for, you know."

I roll onto my back and stare up at the ceiling. "I was just thinking." I smooth my hands across my face and rest them either side of my cheeks. "I'm thirty years old and single again."

He moves to lie beside me in silence as he waits for me to go on. I turn my head, dropping my arms beside me, and look up at him.

"I want so much to be a mum one day, not wishing to sound dramatic or anything, but it might not happen for me now." I shrug.

"Oh come on, you can't be serious, Em? You're still young. If kids is what you want then there's years ahead of you for that."

"You're assuming I'll meet someone else and not be decrepit by the time our relationship reaches the point where kids are an option."

He rolls onto his side, pulling me onto mine until our bodies are in line and almost touching. "Look at me." He tilts my head up with my chin. "You will meet someone else if that's what you want."

I look down and he lifts my head up again.

"And you will make a fantastic mum one day, I know it."

A tear lingers in the corner of my eye as he draws me into him. I inhale his smell and I have to stop myself drifting off into past memories.

"This was supposed to distract you, not bring up bad thoughts."

"It hasn't, I'd be thinking these things anyway. We

could talk about you some more, you know; that would distract me."

"Of course it would, Miss Nosey Parker. Fire away."

"So why hasn't some lucky girl snapped you up, mister?" I ask, breaking away from his embrace.

"Oh, you know."

Awaiting his response, I spy forehead wrinkles, which is not something I've noticed on him before. Neither of us is getting any younger.

"Girls have always been more interested in my future title, the estate, or my money."

I know Chris always used to talk about how fickle people could be, though I didn't know he still felt that way.

"Well, you know I've always been friends with you for your … actually, I don't know why we're friends. I should probably leave."

He launches his fingertips into my ribcage.

"No, please!" I squeal for mercy.

Chris releases me and I spring to my feet.

"Come on, it's bedtime," he says with remnants of laughter in his tone.

"What about the game?"

"We can continue tomorrow. I think you could do with some rest. You okay?" he asks when we reach the door, giving me a goodnight hug.

"I am now," I reply.

Chapter 4

I'm sitting in a square lounge, on a low-down green sofa, opposite a small wooden surround fireplace with a granite hearth, upon which sits a bowl full of tiny seashells. To my left is my middle-aged male counsellor on a cream chair, to my right ticks an analogue alarm clock that he uses to time the appointments.

I've been attending counselling for the past four months, in the hope that life might make some sense again. Much to my surprise, it's working and this is to be my last session. To quote my counsellor: I no longer seem like a person that something is happening to. I'm now a person that something *has* happened to. My life makes a lot more sense than it did a few months ago, so I agree with his assessment. I can't deny there are still some dark days, but despite the rollercoaster of the past few months, my world no longer seems upside-down and days are about living, not just existing.

It's helped being home with my parents and having the support and friendship of Chris and Lucy. In fact, I'm not sure I would have survived without Chris in particular. He knows me better than anyone does, and in the past few months our friendship has gone back in time.

"What's new?" My counsellor's standard opening question. He never opens with, 'How are you?' Mostly because it often proved too hard a question to answer back in the days when I didn't really know how I was from one day to the next.

"Nothing much this week."

"I bet you're enjoying the nice weather? It must be nice to run in something other than the rain?" he says.

"It is, though I've kind of become accustomed to the elements."

I run in all weather. The sun gives me an extra spring in my step, the rain refreshes my senses, and the wind makes me dig deep, pushing my body to find out what I'm capable of. No matter how bad the day, as soon as I lace up my trainers and start to run I feel the stress and strains lift from me. It helps me sleep. It makes me hungry, which means that I no longer look emaciated. In fact, I'm in the best shape of my life from all the exercise. Running has given me a purpose. Sometimes it's given me a reason to get up, or simply leave the house. When people around me suggested antidepressants to help my low mood, I chose running.

"Well, you're looking really well. Much healthier than when we first met, which is fantastic to see," he adds.

"Thank you, I feel healthier."

"So, how are you, Emma?" he finally asks.

"I'm fine. It's been a good week." I'm sitting with

my arms and legs crossed, my usual position. It pleases me the question is no longer hard to answer. These days I am fine, most of the time.

"What's been good about it?"

"Nothing special. I suppose it's just been normal. I used to take *normal* for granted before this."

"Okay." My counsellor nods.

This is his response when he wants me to elaborate. If I don't he'll simply continue to probe until I do.

"At one point I suppose the pain and sadness felt as if it would never end. I thought I would always feel that heartbroken. Now, I feel as if there's more to life again." I pause, playing with my necklace.

"Go on." He removes his glasses and rests them on his crossed knee.

I shuffle. "I like that I don't feel angry anymore. I know now that it didn't change anything, it just made me feel worse. It's good not to carry that around every day."

"I think we reflected, last time, that anger is a perfectly reasonable emotion to go through, but that it's healthy for you to recognise its effect on you," he replies.

There was a great deal of 'reflecting back' on my own thoughts or our mutual observations made during sessions. It's helped me to separate the narrative from the more important issues that I needed to deal with. The narrative, which was what my counselling sessions had consisted of in the early days, was about telling the story and mainly used as an outlet for my emotions.

The reflections were about seeing how I could deal with those emotions, process them, and move forward. My counsellor is good at making a distinction between the two and he's been teaching me to do the same.

As usual, I observe the painting above the fireplace. In it, five faint seagulls are flying in an orange sky towards a distant setting sun. The waves of the dark green sea beneath them foam, the spray of which reaches high as they crash against one another. I feel as if I know every inch of this painting, as if it represents my emotional journey somehow. Sometimes, I've stared at the painting feeling as though the sea in the picture may engulf me, often willing it to. At other times, the relentless vigour of the raging sea represented all of my emotions: denial, anger, depression, as they collided with one another, vying for my attention. What I'd envied most in the painting was the flight of the seagulls clear above in the sky, fleeing the storm around them. Today, though, the painting appears different to me, as if I'm seeing it more clearly. The sun isn't setting, it's breaking through the clouds and allowing light to shine on the sea below. The seagulls are not fleeing the storm as I'd once thought, they are dancing defiantly above the water, knowing that the storm will soon pass and they will be able to land on the peaceful ocean and resume life as it was before.

I know that my life will never be as it was before the storm. I'm a different person now, but as far as I can tell, I've all but weathered the worst of it. What's more, I've learnt to dance defiantly above my situation just like the seagulls in the painting, with strength I never knew I had.

Realising my counsellor is still waiting for me to continue, I do.

"I know how far I've come," I say. "I've realised something from all our conversations. I was unhappy even before my husband left me. I was settling for a life I didn't enjoy and it was always in the back of my mind how lonely I might be one day, despite being married. Now, finally, I feel as if I have my life back, however much I couldn't see it to start with. It's my second chance at happiness and I'm ready for it."

"That's good to hear you say, Emma." He returns his glasses to the bridge of his nose. "What's next?"

"I've started my new job at the hospital, which means I'll soon be able to rent somewhere on my own."

"That's fantastic. Getting your independence back is a positive step. How do you feel about being back at work after your time off?"

"It's daunting. I won't pretend it's not. I work in A&E, so it's back to crazy long shifts and being super busy. It'll be fun to work with my friend Jo again, though."

"Well, it will certainly add to your sense of normality. We talked about this being our last session, how are you feeling about that?"

A wave of apprehension washes over me. These sessions have been my lifeline these past four months. Being able to talk with someone who is neutral and unbiased has helped me process emotions and address issues I never knew I had.

"I think I'm ready."

"Well, as you've already reflected on today, you've come a long way, Emma. Should you ever need to come back then just book in with my secretary. I have every confidence you'll be just fine." He casts me a sincere smile.

It's odd seeing him shuffle to the end of the sofa as he does at the end of every session. He's seen me through one of the toughest times in my life and I've bared so much of my soul to him, yet I will most likely never see him again.

"Thank you for everything." I resist the urge to hug him. Scooping up my bag from the floor, I put it over my shoulder and take one final look at the painting before leaving the room.

"Bye then."

"Bye, Emma. Take care."

It's a beautiful day and I can feel the subtle warmth of early summer sunshine on my face as I step outside. I feel as if I've partially sleepwalked through the past months of my life. One minute I was arriving back at my parents' farm in the cold January wind and the next it's already May. There are things to look forward to and I'm the most excited I've been in a long time about tonight's ball. It's my favourite longstanding tradition at the estate, the Annual May Charity Ball, which began in the sixties when the family established the charitable trust that now owns and runs the estate.

Up until when I was old enough to attend, I used to have a sleepover with Stephen, Chris and Lucy at the house. The nanny always looked after us, which meant my parents could enjoy their evening at the ball also. From the age of about seven, we started our own tradition of waiting for the nanny to fall asleep, which she could promptly be relied upon for, and then we would creep out to sit at the top of the grand staircase. We watched through the wooden banister railings as guests arrived. I'd marvelled at the ladies in spectacular ball gowns in every style and colour, and the gentlemen in crisp dinner jackets who escorted them. It was the epitome of romantic. I would close my eyes and sway my head to the rhythm of the string quartet and imagine being downstairs, dancing the night away like all the other guests. With Stephen and Chris looking on and poking fun at us, Lucy would pull me to my feet and we would spin and swirl, holding out our nightdresses as if they were ball gowns. The year that Lucy and I turned sixteen, we were finally allowed to attend. Our excitement meant that planning for it began a good six months in advance. Looking back, it was more intense than planning for a wedding.

I remember back to that day, sitting around in our dressing gowns in Lucy's bedroom listening to the latest Backstreet Boys album, hot rollers in our hair as we painted our nails to match the colour of our dresses.

"I really hope I get asked to dance tonight!" Lucy says.

I giggle nervously.

"I don't think I'd know what to do if someone asked me to dance."

"Honestly, Ems," Lucy says, frustrated. "You dance with them. Just let them lead, okay?"

"But my parents will be there. It'll be so embarrassing."

Lucy shakes her head, far more confident than I, especially with boys. She already has a boyfriend from school.

"Is Michael coming tonight?"

I watch as Lucy's toe separators make her walk like a penguin over to the CD player to change the music.

"No way!" Lucy scrunches up her face. "I'm keeping my options open. Besides, some of Stephen's mates are coming. Thought I might try an older man," she says, casting me a look over her shoulder, trying to seem sophisticated.

Two hours, a few layers of lipstick and a can of hairspray later, we are standing in front of the mirror admiring our handiwork. Lucy's wearing a short, hot pink organza dress with a sweetheart neck, black heels, and clutch to match. I'm wearing a long, baby blue satin dress with spaghetti straps, a silver pashmina draped around my shoulders and matching purse in my hand.

"We look hot!" Lucy sways from side to side admiring our reflections.

I'm unsure the word 'hot' can be used to describe me. I've daydreamed for years about walking down the grand staircase wearing a stunning dress, with Prince Charming there to greet me with a kiss on my hand. In reality, I'm wearing a pretty dress, not a stunning one like Lucy. I have a boyish figure and braces, and I'm in no danger of Prince Charming waiting anywhere for me.

With the memory still making me smile, I hang my car keys behind the door in my parents' kitchen and pull out my phone.

"Hello."

"Hey, Luce, you busy?"

"I'm actually about to collect my dress for tonight. Want to join me?"

"Sounds great," I say.

"Where are you?" Lucy asks.

"At home."

"Be there in ten."

With that, the phone goes dead.

Shopping with Lucy is like shopping with a professional. She's fast, decisive, and loves to spend ridiculous amounts of money. Like the time when she ordered a designer handbag online and spent nearly nine hundred pounds with one click of a button. I didn't have that sort of money, nor did I think I could ever justify spending that amount on a handbag. Lucy and I may be very different, but I love her all the same.

Ten minutes later, as promised, she's honking the horn of her baby pink Audi TT outside the front door. It's the world's most impractical car to own when living in the middle of the countryside, but that doesn't seem to bother her. I have to admit, I love it almost as much as she does.

"Hi," I greet her, climbing down into the car, feeling as if my legs are all of a sudden up by my chin. "I forget how low down these seats are."

"You always say that." Lucy leans over and kisses my cheek. "How are you?"

"I'm good," I say and realise I mean it for the first time in a long time, "I had my last counselling session this morning."

"You graduated. Congrats." Lucy pulls out of the driveway. "Does that mean we're celebrating?"

"Absolutely." I beam.

"Well, we can start by buying you an expensive dress to wear tonight, followed by lunch. All my treat," Lucy announces.

"I have …"

"Don't tell me you have a dress already, Emma Millar, because I know what you're like. We are not recycling a former party outfit this year, so no arguments."

I don't attempt another protest.

The boutique shop in the next town has a gastropub nearby owned and run by a former MasterChef finalist, who's an old friend of Lucy's. The pub is always fully booked weeks in advance, but we often stopped there for lunch, after shopping, along with a glass of prosecco—as is tradition. The boutique itself sells chic designer dresses and shoes, including some fabulous Jimmy Choos. Hence, why it's one of Lucy's personal favourites and she shops there like she's on commission.

From the second we enter the shop door, it's like we're recreating a scene from *Pretty Woman.* Sales assistants flock around us and pander to our every whim. The only thing missing is Richard Gere, or pizza, I find myself thinking, realising how hungry I am.

Circumventing the attention, I move around the room and look at the various styles of dresses. There's the usual sections: bridal, ball gowns, cocktail dresses and the aforementioned designer dresses. No doubt where Lucy's is from. My eyes are drawn to an ivory-coloured, satin wedding dress with a sweetheart neckline just like I wore on my wedding day. I run my fingers over the gathered mid-section of beaded fabric and try to ignore the memories it conjures.

"Emma," Lucy calls out.

"Have you seen anything you like?"

"I'm still looking," I reply. Deciding it's safer to pick out my own dress, I begin scanning the rails more earnestly.

Settling on two styles of dress to try on, I enter the exquisite changing room. Soft white lighting highlights the fleck of gold in the wallpaper, and behind the thick cream fabric curtain stands a pale gold chaise longue where I drape the dresses. I remove my clothes in awe of my surroundings. This is the first time I've been this side of the curtain, as I'm normally a spectator to Lucy. I slip a pale pink A-line strapless dress over my thighs and zip it up. As I draw back the curtain, I see Lucy standing on a pedestal, an assistant fluffing the bottom of her stunning purple strapless dress.

Lucy swivels around and wrinkles up her nose disapprovingly at the dress I'm wearing. She, however, looks incredible in hers, if not a little edgy. Her dress is floor length at the back and short, being somewhat of an understatement, at the front.

"Wow, Luce! That dress is amazing."

"Are you sure?"

"Absolutely," I say, but know she doesn't need my approval, nor will she mind if she doesn't have it.

"I love it!" She turns side to side, with her hands on her hips.

"Yours is terrible, go try something else on," Lucy orders.

I salute.

"Cheeky!" I hear her call from behind me.

My next dress is a Jenny Packham chiffon, V-neck evening gown, with capped sleeves, in a colour best described as peacock. It's completely covered with lace and beadwork and as soon as I put it on I realise it is quite possibly the most beautiful dress I've ever worn. It clings delicately to my waist and feels silky against my thighs. As I reappear, standing tall, I hear the store assistants make gushing sounds.

"Perfect!" Lucy signals for me to turn and I oblige. "Emma, that dress makes your eyes look fiercely green."

I touch the fabric around my waist with my fingertips and turn my head to see the back of the dress in the mirror as Lucy joins me.

"We're going to rock it tonight," she says, letting out a little squeal of excitement, causing one assistant to jump as she approaches us.

"Here you are, Miss Golding, champagne-coloured Jimmy Choo Vamps." The store assistant presents Lucy with the shoes.

"Oh, no, they're for Emma." She signals towards me.

I receive them as though they're the crown jewels. The light bounces off them and they sparkle like nothing I've seen before, aside from Lucy's one carat Leo diamond engagement ring. Sitting back on the chaise longue, I slip them one at a time onto my feet. My dress falls over them as I stand, so I hitch it up at the front and rotate my ankle to see them from every angle.

"Lucy, these are beautiful, but too much."

"Nonsense." She wafts her hand mid-air. "We'll take both dresses and the Jimmy Choos, thank you." She hands the store assistant her credit card.

I go back to the changing room and reluctantly peel off my dress, keeping the Jimmy Choos on for as long as possible. Tonight can't come soon enough.

Chapter 5

I make my way carefully through the corridors of the house, getting used to wearing my Jimmy Choos. They're so high and I'm not used to heels. Standing still in the changing rooms was one thing; walking in them is an entirely different matter. While the thick carpet is helping, I can't say the same about the sections of wooden flooring I've passed, where I almost slipped over twice.

So much of the house has changed over the years to keep up with it being essentially a place for tours, not to mention a popular and highly sought-after wedding venue, for which Lucy is the wedding and events coordinator—never was there a job more perfect for a person. There's one particularly charming wedding reception room which boasts a stunning view of the river through a double row of lime trees. Within the grounds, there's a beautiful church, perfect for wedding ceremonies. All of Chris's family have been married there, and undoubtedly, it's where Lucy will marry her fiancé Fynn in the near future.

Passing through a series of doors into the north

wing of the house, I walk a long corridor with a deep red carpet that exposes the wooden floors at either side. The shortest route is to cut through the gallery, home to an extensive art collection, some of which is 17th Century, though depleted over the years by inheritance tax—an impressive collection, nonetheless. It's also a room where the Goldings' ancestors line the walls. I pause in front of the picture of Chris's late grandfather, whom he resembles most in his family in both looks and spirit. He died of a heart attack in his early eighties, just two years ago. I was very fond of him and I think the feeling was mutual. His wife, Chris's grandmother, I'm a little less fond of. A feeling which is most certainly also mutual.

I reach the top of the grand staircase and smooth down the front of my dress. My swept-up hair exposes glistening diamond earrings to match my teardrop necklace, which I adjust so it hangs centrally on my neckline. I look to my left, towards the spot where we sat as children and feel every bit as excited now as I had back then. Facing forwards, I see Chris's parents greeting guests in the hall below, putting on a good show. Sir Richard shaking men's hands and Elizabeth kissing the women on their cheeks. I admire him greatly for remaining faithfully in love with his wife, despite their troubles.

Lucy and Fynn are holding hands, and despite how stunning she looks, I think it will be interesting to see what Granny makes of her attire. As the youngest and only girl, she enjoys pushing the boundaries with her edgy fashion sense and by shocking everyone with her less than stereotypical choice of future husband. James Fynn, of no title or fortune, is a local school teacher by profession. Everyone called him by his second name at school and since then it has stuck. Certain antiquated members of the Golding family may disapprove of her choice. However, one person who would have approved was Stephen. They both shared the same selfless and down-to-earth demeanour.

I inhale as my hand finds the banister, hoping I make it down the stairs without falling to my certain death in these heels. *I exaggerate a little.* With more poise than I've ever mustered in my life, I glide down each step feeling as if both the dress and shoes deserve my best efforts. As my fingers trace the wood, its cool smoothness calms my nerves. Part way down, I allow my eyes to lift from my footing to notice Chris has moved to the base of the staircase and is waiting for me. His dark blond, boxer layer hair cut tamed stylishly with wax and his white shirt looks crisp against his black dinner jacket.

Chris holds out his hand for me to take once I reach the bottom.

"Wow." He kisses my hand, eyes locked on my dress. "You look stunning."

"Thank you." I feel warmth rise up into my cheeks. "You look pretty dapper yourself, Mr Golding. Very James Bondesque."

He lifts his chin skyward, readjusting his bow tie, before signalling to a waiter who presents a silver tray with his white-gloved hand. Chris retrieves two glasses of champagne.

"Cheers." He hands me a glass.

"Cheers." I raise mine and smile.

An eruption of laughter breaks out behind us and I notice Lucy beckoning me from across the room.

"Oh, I'm being summoned by Luce." I lift my eyebrows.

"I assume you've seen *the dress*?" Chris asks.

"I have, and it's gorgeous."

Chris regards me with suspicion.

"But very Lucy," I concede.

"Oh it's very Lucy all right. Just wait until Gran sees it."

"Sees what, Christopher?" Granny appears as if by a puff of smoke beside us.

"Good evening, Grandmother." He kisses her cheek. "You look lovely, as always."

"I look old. Too old for this kind of thing any longer, but thank you for the compliment," Granny says, readjusting the dark aubergine-coloured handbag on her forearm which matches the colour of her outfit. "Good gracious, what on earth is your sister wearing?" She strains her eyes and wrinkles her nose as if she were holding an absurdly small pair of glasses on the bridge of it.

Chris stifles a laugh. "You know Lucy, Gran, always one to make a statement."

"I think I need a stiff drink," she mutters almost to herself, then sidles off in the direction of a waiter before

I can say a word.

"She's just so …"

"Trying."

"Yeah, but I …"

"Love her, if only sometimes for the fact that she's flesh and blood."

"I've said this before, haven't I?"

"Once or twice." I laugh, placing a hand over my mouth.

I can see another group of guests have taken up Lucy's attention, so I don't rush away.

"Are you hogging this gorgeous woman's attention, Chris?" A familiar dark-haired man slides beside us, draping his arm around Chris's shoulders. "Emma Millar. It's been like … years."

Chris shrugs him off.

"I heard about the divorce. That sucks."

"Andy!" Chris raises his voice.

I touch Chris's arm.

"I no longer cry at the slightest mention of my divorce, so it's starting to suck less, thank you, Andy."

Chris's frame is rigid and there's a moment of silence in our group.

"The Harringtons have just arrived, mate." Andy breaks the awkwardness by drawing our attention to the man shaking hands with Sir Richard and the two women stood beside him. Elizabeth is fondly embracing the younger of the two.

I watch a curious exchange between them and the

young woman looks directly at us.

"I need to go and greet people. Will you be okay?" he asks me.

"Of course," I reassure him.

"Behave!" Chris fires a warning shot at Andy.

"Always, mate, always." He smirks.

Shaking his head, Chris walks towards the woman, and what I now assume are her parents. He embraces her, kissing her cheek.

"I'm sorry things didn't work out with Matt, Emma," Andy says, tilting his head to one side, a gesture I find more amusing than irritating these days. "It may be little consolation, but he was a fool to let you go."

"Thank you." I smile, appreciating the sincerity in his tone.

"Would you like to dance?" He mock bows, holding out his hand like someone from a Jane Austen novel. When he glances back up at me, I feel as though I might dissolve in the warmth of his cognac-coloured eyes. A flutter in my stomach, resembling nerves or excitement, takes me by surprise.

"Why, thank you." I take his hand and curtsy.

We dance in time with the music, slow enough so I can take in the surroundings of one of my favourite rooms in the house. Statues of Greek mythological figures stand in niches around the room, between spherical pillars running high up towards the ceiling. A large autumnal leaf print in the centre of the floor, encased by a golden border, reflects the light of three glimmering chandeliers above.

“Are you still in touch with Melissa?” he asks.

“Not since we left school.” I narrow my eyes. “I’m surprised you’d want to talk about her.”

“Ah, that’s ancient history.”

“Yeah, but I remember how cut up you were. In fact, it was the first time I considered you had a heart.”

He lets go of my arm and grips his chest. “I can’t believe you can say such things.”

We laugh in sync.

“We were young and I totally see why she ran off with Toby what’s his chops.”

“To be fair, we could all see that. Not the leaving you part, just him being the Italian heartthrob that he was.” I grimace.

He makes a manly cough sound, puffing out his chest.

“I didn’t know I was going to need a shield dancing with you.”

“A shield?”

“Yeah, to protect my ego. You’re destroying it!”

“Ha-ha-ha.” I shake my head and relax into his arms. I watch his confident familiar features and enjoy the feel of his body as he holds me tight around my waist.

“I lost track of you when you went to uni,” I say.

“You can’t say that disappointed you too much? You hated me at school.”

“I didn’t hate you.” I purse my lips to one side.

He nods, slowly, and says nothing, or at least not with his mouth.

"Okay, so you weren't my favourite person in the world … but then you did spend half your time drooling over Lucy and the rest of the time teasing me mercilessly."

He dips me and I inhale.

"I would have *drooled* over you, too, if that's what we're calling it, but you used to seethe whenever you saw me. It was a little off-putting."

This was news to me and I feel completely disarmed. Andy had made a beeline for Lucy at school, though Chris had warned him off. He had never seemed remotely interested in me.

"You would not." I laugh.

He just looks at me.

"… So, do you still work in London?" I ignore the intensity of his stare and try to control the blush rising from my neckline to my cheeks.

"I just finished uni again actually," he says.

Raising my eyebrows, I pause to examine him.

"I got my business degree, then got bored working as a suit in London, so I went back to uni to do a farm management course. I moved back home a couple of months ago."

"Wow, I didn't know farming interested you?"

"I didn't either until I helped out on a mate's farm for a couple of weeks one summer." He smiles. "You still nursing?"

"I am."

"Are you back working at City?"

"Yes."

"Look at us. I always thought you'd be the farmer, not me."

"I thought I would, too, so did my parents. They hoped I would take over the farm one day when they retire, or better still, I'd marry a farmer who would. So you could say I'm somewhat of a disappointment in that area."

"From what I remember of your parents I find it hard to believe they would ever be disappointed in you. So what stopped you taking on the farm?"

"Matt. He was a city boy. His work was down in Kent and so I followed him. Long, lonely hours in a warm tractor cab wasn't really his thing."

"What was his thing?"

"Trips to Europe, nice suits, fancy cars … and other women, as it turns out."

He raises an eyebrow, though doesn't comment.

"I suppose by the time the novelty of him wore off, I was in too deep. I just thought we'd make a go of it, you know, and I tried … anyway, enough about that."

All of a sudden, the pace of the music changes and he spins me around until I'm dizzy and laughing so fiercely I can't breathe. When he releases me, I rest by a pillar, panting for breath, my skin hot and glistening.

"You dance very well," I say.

"Dance lessons." He's breathing harder still. "My mum made me have lessons when I was younger."

I try not to snigger at the thought of Andy as a boy being made to take dance lessons, but fail.

"I know, I know. I protested, but she insisted that

women love men who can dance."

"She was right." I turn my head away from him and look out over the dance floor. Flirting with him isn't intentional, though it does feel good.

"So, are you back in Pineham for good?" he asks.

I don't hear him at first as I notice Chris dancing with the woman from before. A petite, red-haired beauty.

"Em?"

"Sorry, what?"

He laughs. "Are you planning on staying in Pineham now?"

"Yes, maybe." I pause, then realise my vagueness isn't an answer. "Sorry, I guess I'm not sure." I smile, my attention back with him.

"Well, you don't have to decide now, do you? I have to say, though, moving home is one of the best things I've done with my life since I left school. I love it here."

"I love it too. I've just got used to a different sort of life in Kent, that's all. I'm not sure I'm ready to slip back into what my parents' ideal for my life is."

"Marrying a farmer and running their farm with him?"

"Something like that."

"Sorry, I didn't mean anything by that."

"I know."

His sensitivity surprises me. He didn't seem like the same boy I used to know. His self-assurance is more charming, as though he's refined it into an attractive quality as a man. Perhaps there's a vulnerable side to him hiding behind all his bravado, which I can't help but like.

"I should be off," he says. "I only came to show my face."

"Are you not staying here tonight?"

He flashes me one of his smiles and I melt a little. The effect he's having on me makes me feel uneasy, as does the thought of him leaving already.

"I'm helping a friend on his farm in Lincolnshire tomorrow, so I'm off down there tonight ready for the early start."

I wrinkle my nose. "Well, thank you for the dance."

"My pleasure."

He hovers in the brief moment of silence between us and I feel myself freeze. Then he leans in and kisses my cheek.

"Goodnight," he whispers in my ear.

My whole body feels as though an electrical current is surging through me and it doesn't stop until it reaches my toes. "Goodnight," I say and lean against the cold pillar as I watch him walk away.

The evening ends before I'm ready for it to. Andy is still very much in my mind as I retreat to one of the lounges just before midnight. I sink into the cream sofa, which absorbs my tired body. It's been so long since I've felt a spark I was starting to imagine it was no longer possible for someone to make me feel this way. I close my eyes and remember how Andy's breath on my cheek felt as he whispered in my ear.

"So, this is where you've been hiding?" Chris is leaning on the doorframe, his top shirt button undone and his tie hanging loosely around his neck.

I flinch. "I'm too wired to go to bed yet. All the champagne, I think."

He widens his eyes.

"You're safe. I'm pretty sober."

"Phew!"

I reach down, removing my Jimmy Choos one at a time, and wiggle my toes into the thick cream carpet, enjoying how comforting it is. Keeping them on all night was worth every blister.

Chris joins me on the sofa. "I was thinking, how about we watch a film in the cinema room, like old times?"

"Sure, just let me get changed first."

"Okay, meet you in there?" he says.

Clutching my shoes and purse, I make my way through the maze of once familiar corridors to my room. My suite is stunning, with the traditional ceiling roses and chandelier preserved. The old wooden shutters have been removed from the windows and in their place are cream roman blinds and voile curtains, swept to one side. Against a blue damask wallpaper feature wall there's a modern upholstered angel bed, which I can't wait to climb in to. So much so that I almost change my mind about meeting Chris to watch a film.

As much as I love to dress up, it's equally satisfying to take everything off at the end of the evening and be comfortable. Especially on a night as warm as this one, thanks to an early May heatwave. I slip into a pair of shorts and pull a T-shirt over my securely pinned-up hair. I consider removing them, but then I remember how many the hairdresser put in and I think better of it.

A few wrong turns later and I find the cinema room in the corridor next to the family apartments.

"Hey," I say as I enter.

Chris has changed, too, and is sitting on the sofa, his toned, tanned legs stretched out in front of him, searching through films.

"I thought you'd got lost."

"Not quite, though if you change much more of the house I won't know my way around." I giggle. "The suite is beautiful, by the way."

He dips his head. "Thank you. I was hoping you'd like it."

"It's a happy mix of modern vs traditional, how could I not?"

"Well, that means a lot."

"I'm so impressed with all that the estate has achieved in the past few years. It seems to grow more successful year upon year."

"We had over one hundred thousand visitors last year, and that doesn't include private functions such as weddings. At least it is safe in the family's hands for a few more years, if it keeps up."

"I have every faith it will be, with you in charge."

"I have a lot of help, and a board of trustees keeping a very close eye on me. Not to mention my father."

I tilt my head and pull at my hair.

"You okay?"

"I have thousands of pins in my hair and it's starting to make my head hurt."

"Thousands, huh?"

I pick up a cushion and fling it at his head. He ducks and laughs, tapping the sofa next to him for me to sit down.

"Let me." He lifts his hands and begins gently sliding pins from my hair, one by one.

I let out a long breath and wriggle my shoulders.

"What shall we watch?" he asks. "Please don't say *The Notebook*."

"I wasn't going to say *The Notebook*. I wouldn't jeopardise you playing it at the film festival." I twist my head to smile at him, but he turns it back again, so he can continue untangling a strand of hair.

"You always say, '*The Notebook*'. Besides, it's too late to change the line-up now. It's already on the website and advertisements."

"I know I've seen, very cool. How's it all going?"

"I've been pretty busy these past few weeks with non-film festival stuff, so there's still plenty to do. I'll sort it, though."

"I can help some more, if you like?"

"I might have to take you up on that."

"I'd be happy to," I say, turning my attention to

the screen and taking over the job of searching for a film. The cinema room has two L-shape silver sofas in front of a wide screen. The carpet is grey, as are the walls, lit with dimmable spotlights.

"Aww! *While You Were Sleeping*."

"Are you kidding me? It's a Christmas film and it's like twenty-five degrees outside."

"It's not a Christmas film," I argue.

"Oh, I must be confusing it with another film about snow, Christmas, and that actor with the big bushy eyebrows."

"Peter Gallagher?"

"Him, yes."

"There's also Sandra Bullock and we know how much you love her …" I give him my best puppy dog eyes.

"Put it on," he says through gritted teeth.

"Really?"

"Yep. Besides, I've got my work cut out untangling your hair."

"Thousands of pins, huh?"

"Touché."

I don't need to see his face to know he's smiling.

With my hair now free from pins, I relax into the cushions. As if reading my mind, he reaches down the side of the sofa and produces a bag of Kettle crisps, Galaxy counters, and two bottles of water.

"You're very prepared as always, Mr Golding."

"You have me well trained, Miss Millar," he says,

handing me the snacks.

Crossing my legs, I offer him the now open packet of crisps.

"It's been a while since we've done this," he says.

"Yeah, it has." I rub my temple.

"Your head still sore?"

"I've got a headache is all."

"Here, *lightweight*." He passes me a bottle of water. "Drink this."

I scowl playfully, taking it from him, and when I'm done, he places a cushion in his lap and taps it. Shuffling towards him, I place my head on the pillow and he begins to roll his thumbs around my forehead.

"So you spent a lot of time with Andy tonight?"

I fidget. "I guess so." I keep my eyes closed. The film's almost over, but I can still follow it, having seen it hundreds of times.

"Is that it?" His fingers pull at the skin in the nape of my neck.

"What do you want me to say? We talked. We danced." I open my eyes and see the look on his face. "Okay, maybe having some male attention wasn't exactly unpleasant. It's been a while …" His look changes and I can't read it so easily.

"Well, I think he likes you, so you can have as much attention there as you want."

"I admit it's nice to feel something again, but that doesn't mean I know what I want. No one's given me butterflies for a very long time."

"Butterflies, hey."

"Don't start."

"I wasn't. Do you think you'll see him again?"

"I think so." I fling my hands to my face. "What am I saying? It's Andy! You know how much he irritated me when we were younger."

Chris says nothing.

"What are you not saying?"

"You've said it yourself, it's Andy." Chris appears to be trying to find the right words. "I love him as a mate, but be careful is all I'll say."

"I'm not planning on marrying the guy. Besides, I'm pretty sure polygamy is illegal in the UK."

"You're really annoying!" He pokes me playfully. "But seriously, just say the word and I'll warn him off you again."

I tilt my head back to look at him.

"You warned him off me before? I thought that was just Luce?"

"I warned him off both of you. He's a typical bloke. Always was, always will be. I cared about you too much."

"Cared, as in past tense?"

"Care, as in past, present, and future. You know I do," he says.

In our silence, I hear the last lines of the film and turn my head to the screen.

Chris sighs.

"Sigh of relief that the torture's over?"

"Nope, that film gets me *every* time," he says with a smirk.

Teasing him, I hand him a tissue.

"Ha-ha. Well done, Witty." He whips the cushion from under my head and covers my face with it. "Time for bed," he says.

I stretch and yawn. "That giant bed is definitely calling me. Thanks for the head massage."

"No problem."

"Night, Buddy." I blow him a kiss as I reach the door.

"Night, Em."

Chapter 6

"Hey, I came straight over when I got your text. You okay?"

I'm standing in my bedroom, shuffling from one foot to the other. Seeing my reflection in the mirror, I look pale. Chris and I have barely seen one another since he got back from his latest lads holiday in Ibiza. Not that I've had the opportunity, with how much time Matt and I have been spending together since we started dating.

"I need to tell you something," I say, closing my eyes.

Chris comes over, holding the tops of my arms.

"I'm getting married."

He releases me and steps back, his posture stiffening.

Moments pass, I'm not sure how long. All I know is the room appears smaller all of a sudden as I wait for him to speak.

"Say something," I plead.

"Wow!" He exhales with full force.

"Is that it?"

He takes a deep breath. "When did this happen?"

"Matt asked me last night."

Chris isn't smiling. He doesn't seem happy, which is unsurprising because neither do I. Announcing your engagement should be a happy conversation, done together, with people congratulating us.

My gaze lands on every part of the room except on him, sensing he's suspicious that I've not told him the whole story. And I haven't.

"You've only been together a couple of months. Do you not think you should …?"

"I'm pregnant!"

He recoils, wide-eyed, the missing piece suddenly falling into place.

My insides feel as though they may plummet to my feet. "Please say something, anything …" I touch his arm, tears rolling down my cheeks. "Tell me you're happy for me, Chris?"

His jaw clenches as he looks at me and instinctively he holds out his arms for me to walk into.

"I'm happy for you," he whispers by the side of my cheek. "If this is what you want then I'm happy for you."

"I'm scared," I say and feel his grip on me tighten.

I jolt awake, covered in cold sweat. It's not the first bad dream I've had in the past few months, but it's been years since I've replayed that memory. Chris found himself that summer for the first time since his brother's death. I, on the other hand, remember it as the summer I lost myself.

It's the morning after the ball. Chris and I stayed up so late I almost didn't bother surfacing at all. Realising how rude it would seem if I didn't, I enter the breakfast room with trepidation. Being greeted by them at the ball, and sitting down to breakfast with the family, are two very different things.

Sir Richard, as always, is at the head of the table reading a newspaper, with Chris sat beside him. Elizabeth and Granny are finishing their toast. Everyone looks up, smiling as I enter. Granny sort of purses her lips, which for her amounts to the same thing.

"Good morning," I say.

"Good morning," a small chorus of voices return.

Chris pours himself a coffee, holding up a cup for my benefit.

"Yes please," I reply, with a nod.

Sir Richard rests his newspaper in front of him as I go over and kiss his cheek.

"Nice to have you here," he says as I take my seat beside Granny.

"Did you sleep well, Emma?" Elizabeth asks from across the table.

"Yes, thank you. The suite is beautiful and the bed is quite possibly the comfiest I've ever slept in."

"I'm pleased you like it," she says, before sipping tea from her china teacup.

"Morning, everyone." Lucy breezes in.

"You're very bright and breezy this morning, young lady," Sir Richard notes.

She takes her seat, pouring herself some coffee. "I'm just happy, that's all."

"Any particular reason for that?" I enquire of my friend.

"Fynn and I've set a date for the wedding!"

I jump up and rush over to hug her.

"Congratulations, Sis," Chris says, joining me, though the rest of the room does not follow in the happy gestures.

"Is the ink even dry on his divorce papers?" Granny pipes up.

There's a loud clatter as Elizabeth catches her teacup after almost knocking it off the saucer.

"We love one another, Gran." Lucy's tone is indignant.

"When?" Elizabeth asks.

"August."

"That's very soon. How shall you be ready in time?"

"It will be fine, Mother."

Lucy had drifted in like a helium-filled balloon, and now with every passing second, she looks more and more deflated.

Chris and I take our seats.

"I still don't know what's wrong with women today. Don't they know how to keep their husbands happy anymore?" Granny rises and retires to an armchair in the back of the room. Not before she casts a disapproving eye over me.

"Granny!" Lucy glowers at her grandmother, and now all that is left of the balloon is crumpled foil.

"Well, it seems that people today see marriage as a dispensable commodity to be thrown away like a pair of old shoes." She continues her tirade. "In my day you stuck at it, made it work. None of this trade in for a younger or richer model business."

"Not that I need to justify myself, or Fynn for that matter, but his wife left him." Lucy's standing, tapping her left foot frantically on the floorboards beneath her.

I sink lower in my chair, my face a darker shade of red than any blushing I'd done last night at the ball.

"I think that's enough, Mother," Sir Richard declares in a shrill tone.

Granny just shrugs.

"Congratulations, darling. I'm sure you and Fynn will be very happy with one another," he says and Lucy gives him a half smile.

"Excuse me." I stand and leave the room in haste.

Without stopping, I make my way past the herbaceous borders of the main garden and over to the lion bridge. Reaching the wide iron gate, I look back and see Chris trailing me. As he slows to stand beside me, I'm focused out over the expanse of the river. He leans over to look at the water below, where the bulrushes are standing tall and proud. The fish are swimming deep in the clear water and two swans drift downstream towards the ducks taking flight.

"Sorry I ran out," I say.

"No, I'm sorry, Em, Gran had no right to say those things. You know what she's like."

"I expected it, to be honest … maybe not quite how she put it, but the judgement at least."

"She wasn't judging you, she was just being her

cheerful little self."

"She's right, though. I never wanted any of this for my marriage."

"Exactly. You didn't want it." Chris hops onto the wall to sit and I join him.

"Poor Lucy, though. What a reception to her announcement."

"You know what my family are like. A divorced school teacher isn't high up on the eligible men list."

"I know." I look down.

"They're being narrow-minded. Dad, not so much, he just wants what's best for her. Deep down he knows Fynn makes her happy, but he has Gran to contend with, and Mum these days."

He rests back on his arms, tipping his head back to get the early morning sun on his face. The quiet sound of the water flowing beneath us. Ahead, I can just about make out the herd of fallow deer in the park on the horizon.

"So your little sister is getting married. How'd you feel about that?" I ask.

"I'm happy for her. I like Fynn."

"Yeah, me too. He seems like a really good guy. Not upset that your kid sister's beating you down the aisle?" I ask.

"Hardly."

"We haven't really talked about your love life since I got back." *I'm keen to know about this girl from the ball, but I don't want to ask him outright for some reason.*

"What love life?"

"You don't have to protect me from relationship talk, you know. I'm okay."

He dips his head in acknowledgement.

"Have you dated much since you and Gabrielle broke up?"

"There's been a few dates here and there."

"Do you keep in touch?"

"With Gabby? No," he says with a firm shake of his head. "According to a mutual friend she's engaged to some guy who manages a hedge fund in London, so I think she's doing all right for herself."

"Does that bother you?"

"Not at all. As great as she was, we both knew it wasn't going anywhere long term."

"I forgot you don't seem to do *long term*."

"What's that supposed to mean?"

"Nothing. It's just I've known many women who were interested in you, but no one's ever seemed good enough."

Chris drums his fingers against the wall. "I don't think for a moment anyone's not good enough for me … besides most of the women you talk about were only interested in me for who I am. Christopher Golding. *Future lord of the manor.* Sucked into the fairy tale ideal of the Great British Country Estate. They weren't interested in me for me and they certainly hadn't got a clue how much work's involved in maintaining a place like Wincastle."

"Maybe you should give someone a chance, that's all I'm saying."

"Perhaps … Have you heard from Andy this morning?"

"Nice change of subject."

He smiles, but I don't push my luck. Of all the things we've shared over the years, Chris has always been most cagey about his love life.

"He wants to see me again tonight, actually. Dinner. I was thinking of asking Lucy and Fynn to come along, make it a little bit less datelike. You can come too, if you like?"

"You do realise it's a date, right?"

I scrunch up my face.

"And thank you for the offer, but I'll leave you guys to it. Fifth wheel isn't really my style."

"You don't seem yourself this morning?"

"I'm good," Chris replies. "Tired, but good."

"Are you sure? You can tell me if there's something on your mind?" I touch his arm and I'm taken back to my dream momentarily.

"I'm sure."

Later in the afternoon, I go for a run to clear my head. Tonight I'm going on a date with Andy and every time I think about it, I want to vomit, my mouth goes dry, and my heart has such palpitations I start to self-diagnose heart conditions. My usual route takes me past the little café in the village, where on occasion I stop for breakfast to replace the calories I've just worked hard to burn off. I pass the primary school where Fynn works and smile to myself that Lucy is breaking with tradition by marrying a 'commoner'. I really like Fynn, he's good for Lucy. Somehow, he makes her more grounded and I have to take my hat off to him for that. As I jog up a hill, I pass the village fruit and vegetable cart, meaning I'm halfway through my run. My pace quickens as I think of Chris's mood this morning. He's distracted and clearly determined not to tell me why. Looping back down the dirt track, I notice my dad coming up in the tractor.

"Ey up, darlin'," he calls out from his cab window over the hum of the engine. "Beautiful weather for it."

"Hey, Dad, certainly is. Good day?" I shout back.

"Can't complain any. Sun's out. Not too warm, a drop of rain overnight'd be good, not too much, mind," he says in his warm Derbyshire tone.

I smile.

"Got a minute?" Dad asks me, shutting down his engine so we can hear one another better.

"Sure." I take the opportunity to rest and stretch out my calf muscles, while Dad climbs down from his cab and joins me by the fence.

"How you doing?" I notice his frown lines and the bags under his eyes.

"I'm doing well, Dad."

"It's just your mother worries." He lifts his cap and scratches his head. "I mean you seem more yourself, but I don't know if that's just you putting on a brave face for your old dad?"

"I promise it's not me putting on a brave face." I place my stretched leg on the ground and go up on tiptoes to kiss his cheek.

"Glad to hear it. Right then, best be getting back to it. Enjoy the rest of your run."

With that, he climbs back into his cab and I run off as the sound of the engine roars back to life. My sweet Dad, I think as I pass the back road next to Wincastle, a man of few words but one huge heart.

Wincastle is beautiful at this time of year, the outskirts wild and rural with pink and white apple blossom on the trees and in the hawthorn hedgerow lining the track on which I'm running. The trees are tall and uniform, creating an archway across the long driveway as I near the northern entrance to the estate. The grass is cleanly mowed and the hedges trimmed to perfection. There's a riding school on the left and further up the path a gate and cattle grid. Colin, the head groundsman for many years, would be pleased with how well things look, I muse as I pass.

Over the years Colin, Chris, Lucy, Stephen and I had become friends. Though this had not always been the case. Chris and Stephen, I remember, had spent many a time fleeing a red-faced Colin. While acting like every other child, they would on occasion forget themselves and kick footballs around in one of the many pristine formal landscaped gardens. One time, Stephen beheaded a row of prizewinning roses Colin happened to be pruning. When he requested to see Sir

Richard the next day, they both expected to be hauled in for a telling-off. Instead, Colin had asked for permission to build a treehouse for them in the woodland on the estate. They suspected at the time that this was to keep them away from his flowerbeds, though they didn't object. A treehouse was every boy's dream.

The square treehouse, with apex roof, stands about ten feet off the ground, is complete with wooden ladder and just about enough room for four people inside. Colin had planted climbing roses so that in time they would grow up the sides and make the treehouse blend in with the landscape. It had been a labour of love built to last a lifetime. Quickly, it became our favourite place to hang out. We ate in there, played in there and sometimes even slept in there. That summer had changed all our perceptions of him, and when the treehouse was finished, we found ourselves choosing to spend time with Colin. Chris and I in particular, as he took us under his wing and taught us how to garden. We even planted a vegetable garden together, which was when he told us about his wife, Rose. They had had no children of their own, the sadness of which couldn't be hidden from his face.

They used to live in one of the gatekeepers' cottages at the entrance to the estate, by the road. Their own private garden had a display of roses rivalling any of those in the estate gardens. One day, when we'd been invited back to the cottage for sandwiches and lemonade, Rose told us that Colin loved roses more than he loved her. To which he replied that she was his favourite Rose of them all, kissing her on the cheek. The smile on her face told me this was part of their usual repertoire and something often said to one another. The treehouse hadn't just been built to keep them out of his way, as they'd originally thought, he'd built it because he had no children of his own to build one for.

After a much-needed shower I drive to the nursing home where Colin now lives. As I pass through the reception, I'm not greeted with the smell of festering urine or any other bodily functions, like some of the homes I worked in as a student nurse. It's light and airy and their choice of social events makes my life look dull by comparison. Colin has even taken on keeping the gardens in check at the home, and over the past couple of years, they've bloomed under his watchful eye.

I find him sitting outside with a cup of tea and a book, a familiar picture on my visits with him. Without looking, I know that on the inside cover of his book is a black and white photograph of Rose and him on their wedding day. 'The happiest day of my life,' he would say and show me the photo. There's one thing different today, though, and that's Chris, sitting beside him, chatting away.

"Hello, Emma." Colin tries to stand up when he sees me.

"Hi Col, don't get up." I lean over his stooped frame, hug him, and then do the same with Chris, who is standing. *And they say chivalry is dead.*

"How are you?" I ask Colin.

"You know, there's life in the old boy yet. Most days." He sniggers.

He always says that. Though the past few visits, I've seen a decline in his health. There are braces holding up his trousers, he stoops even lower when he walks and he often tells me things twice. Colin is eighty-four, and up until Rose's death five years ago, never looked a day over seventy.

"That good-for-nothing ex-husband of yours leaving you alone? Never did like the fella …" he mutters the last part, though not quiet enough so that I can't hear him.

"So far so good." I eye Chris, who is stifling a smile.

"Glad my Rosie isn't around to see you as heartbroken as you've been these last few months."

"Fancy a game, you two?" I point to the box of dominoes on the end of the table, trying to divert him from this subject. I worry the stress is no good for him and I'm in such a good place that I don't want to rehash the past.

"Are you sure?" Colin asks, opening the box and tipping out the dominoes on the table. "You've never won yet."

"She never beats me at games either, Col," Chris adds, and I shove him with my elbow.

"What can I say? I'm a glutton for punishment."

Colin did win, more so these days because I let him, though any moves I do have at the games we play I've learnt from him over the years. I feel guilty for barely seeing him for a few years while I lived in Kent.

"I was just asking Christopher where he's been hiding."

"Hiding?"

"Yes, I haven't seen him in the last few weeks."

He goes on without further comment from anyone.

"Probably because the last time he was here I asked when he was going to find himself a girl. I have a 1950 Bordeaux wine in my cupboard that I've been saving for the day any of you had some children." Colin taps a domino on the table as if he were bringing an auction house to attention. "I'm sorry if I sound insensitive, Emma, darling."

I wave my hand nonchalantly. "1950 Bordeaux, though, very nice."

"It was a gift from Chris's grandfather, chosen from his cellar on my own wedding day. We saved a bottle to toast the birth of our first child, but as you know, that was never to be. So we kept it for another happy occasion, then I forgot we had it all these years. Rosie and I had hoped we could celebrate the birth of any of your children, but quite honestly you're all taking too long."

I chuckle and notice Chris scratching his head. Only Colin could say something such as this and it not make me want to cry. "Well, I'm sorry about that.

Lucy may have that one covered, though. She's set the date to marry Fynn, this summer." I place a domino on the table.

"I'm happy about that. Fynn's a decent man." Colin sets a domino down and claps.

"I'm going to lose again, aren't I?"

"Anyway, you came here to tell me something?"

"No, I didn't. I just came to check in. See how you are."

"No, no. Christopher, before Emma got here just now, you were going to tell me something. Let's be having it, before I beat you both at this game and go inside for a lie-down."

"Ah, nothing, Col. I can't even remember what it was now, to be honest, and what's this about you beating me? I'm not planning on letting you win like this one does."

"Hey, I don't let him win, I'm just terrible at games."

"Finally, she admits it!"

"That's hardly fair when you forced my hand!"

"You pair don't change … there!" Colin places his final domino on the table and we both fall silent.

"See, I've still got my wits about me, loves," he says and we erupt with laughter together, just like old times.

Chapter 7

The car's full of Andy's woodsy scent, which is making my stomach clench so tight my organs feel suffocated. Focussing on my breathing isn't helping the situation, it's making me inhale his scent all the more and it's already overwhelming my senses.

"Are you okay?" Andy asks.

"Oh, umm, honestly?" I play with my purse in my lap, "I'm really nervous. It's been a long time since I was last on a date."

He touches the bare skin of my knee and an unfamiliar jolt surges through me.

"Just relax, okay? There's no pressure from me."

"Okay." I breathe out, trying to calm the beating of my heart as Andy's sensitive side continues to surprise me. "I hope you don't mind Lucy and Fynn joining us?"

"No, it's fine. It'll be good to catch up with Fynn. We used to play a bit of cricket in the village back in the day."

"So, how was work this morning?" I ask to kill the awkward pause in conversation.

"Great. Was done by two, so not a bad day's work."

"What exactly were you doing?"

"Peonies."

"Peonies, as in the flower?"

"Yep, my mate grows them on his farm. At this time of year we pick, sort and sell them. They've come in pretty early this year, what with the hot weather."

"I bet you're tired, though, from the early start and all the driving?"

"No, I'm surprisingly awake." He smiles, looking me up and down fleetingly before turning his attention back to the road. This time he doesn't need to touch me for the tingling sensation to return.

All too soon, we pull into The Duck Pond car park alongside Fynn's Range Rover. He turns off the engine and hurries round to the passenger door to open it for me.

"My lady." He mock bows as he did when asking me to dance the night before.

Andy makes gallantry look effortless, which makes me feel more special than I have in a long time.

"Why, thank you," I say as he signals for me to lead the way, leaving me feeling conscious he's checking me out in the blue body-contoured dress Lucy suggested I borrow for the evening.

Lucy and Fynn are in the bar. I notice the ice bucket housing a bottle of prosecco next to her, and Fynn is nursing a pint. As we approach them, she lets out a delighted squeal and jumps up to hug us both in turn.

"I've taken the liberty of ordering us a bottle already." She pours me some fizz. With Lucy it's never what drink would you like? The choice, in her eyes, is always wine, and more often than not, prosecco. Nevertheless, I'm grateful for the drink to help steady my nerves.

"What can I get you, Andy? Do you still drink Guinness?" Fynn asks.

"Yes, mate, that'd be good. I'll come with you." The boys proceed to the bar leaving me to regain my composure.

"You look amaaazing!" Lucy beams.

"Thanks. I feel way too self-conscious in this dress, though."

"Well, you look hot and I don't think Andy's going to want to keep his hands off you."

"Lucy! It's our first date."

"And?"

"Really?"

"I'm just teasing, relax."

I gulp back my drink and promptly pour another.

By the time Fynn and Andy return, the waiter arrives, escorting us to our table in the restaurant. At the centre of the table is a yellow rose in a small crystal vase, sat beside two lit candles burning quietly. I remember the rose had been red the night I'd been here with Chris, mainly because red roses are my favourite.

The air around us fills with wafts of warm bread, rich tomato, and lemon as our starters arrive. I'm feeling hungry now that my nerves are in check, courtesy of the prosecco.

“So, Andy Pandy,” Lucy teases. This had been her pet name for him at school. Seeing his jawline clench, he clearly hates it as much now as he did back then.

“Emma tells me you’re a farmer now? Where are you working at the moment?”

“Yes, Lucy Goosy, I am,” he says, unable to hide the amusement of his own retort.

“Touché.” Lucy nods and they both break with laughter.

“I can see this is going to be fun,” Fynn says.

“Oh, you have no idea,” I say. “Just be thankful, Chris didn’t join us.”

“Why’s that?” Fynn asks.

“Because Andy and Chris would probably order the same meal and see who could finish first, and then when it’s a tie, end it with an arm-wrestling competition.” Lucy laughs.

“Wait a minute!” Andy says. “We weren’t that bad.”

“No, you were worse!” Lucy says. “Especially after Chris managed to beat your goal-scoring record, and take Tammy Chilvers to the school dance in the same week.”

Lucy and I are laughing, holding our sides, as Andy just sits there, shaking his head at us. Fynn pats him on the back.

“In answer to your original question,” he says, not giving either of us the satisfaction of rising to our mockery, "I've been doing bits of work here and there while I get settled."

"I'm sure Mr Millar was only saying the other day that he needs some extra hands on the farm, didn't he, Em?"

What a surprise, Lucy's meddling. And now I'm the one in the firing line.

Andy looks at me, curiously.

"He does normally need extra hands this time of year, yes, Lucy." I send her a wide-eyed 'look' that only she knows means back off, but I know with certainty she won't. In fact, when it comes to Lucy, subtlety is not her strong suit. I once tagged her in a post on Facebook, about friends asking your crush if he likes you, but best friends push you into them and scream 'get some'. This is Lucy.

"I'll ask him for you, see what he thinks," I whisper to Andy, when Lucy is distracted by Fynn.

"Thanks." He looks at me for longer than is comfortable and much to my dismay, I blush.

By the time we've finished our main courses all the tables are occupied around us and as soon as one becomes available, it's promptly filled.

"That was quite possibly the best food I've ever tasted." Andy leans back in his chair, both arms behind his head.

"I'm with you there, mate. How is it that we haven't eaten here before, Luce?" Fynn asks.

"Chris and I used to come here with our parents. I

confess I've forgotten how good it is, but I'm pleased you enjoyed it, baby." She kisses Fynn on his lips and I note how at ease they are in one another's company. I turn away from their PDA to catch Andy staring at me again, and I go to take a sip of my drink, but my glass is empty.

"Another drink, Em?" he offers.

"Can I just have an orange juice, please?" Hearing this, Lucy scrunches up her nose as if she just sucked on a lemon, but I ignore it.

"Sure."

"Thank you." *I don't want to be anything more than tipsy, which I already am.*

"Fynn, Lucy?" he offers.

"Just a Coke for me, please mate? Driving." He signals by turning an imaginary steering wheel mid-air.

"I'll come with," Lucy says, escorting Andy to the bar, not before she winks at me over her shoulder.

As I watch them walk off together, I almost forget Fynn is still beside me.

"Don't worry, I'm sure she's behaving." Fynn leans in to get my attention.

"Oh, I know." I look back at him. "She just loves to matchmake."

He doesn't disagree.

I study him closely for the first time. I've met Fynn on a couple of occasions, though I've not spent much time alone with him. He has a kind face, older looking, but then being eight years her senior, he's certainly ageing well. He's stocky, with light brown hair, trimmed with grey and has a dark tone to his skin, almost Italian looking.

"Are you from round here originally, Fynn?"

"I was born in London, actually."

"That's the twang I can hear."

"Yes, it's only subtle now, but apparently I get quite incoherent when I'm mad."

"Bet the kids at school love that."

"I don't often shout in the classroom, or at all really."

"Yes, you seem like a chilled sort of person. Probably for the best with Luce," I add with a wry smile.

He nods, laughing for a moment, and then his face is more serious. "I'm sorry about your marriage ending. I know it can be a really tough time, especially this whole dating scene."

"Thank you, I'm sorry for you too. I know exactly what you mean. I'm out of practice for sure."

"Yep." He nods, "I felt the same, well that and a bit jaded with it all. Lucy is like a breath of fresh air, though." He glances to where she's standing at the bar.

"You really love her, don't you?"

"I do," was all he had to say to make me believe him.

"I get the feeling Andy's pretty keen on you?"

"No." I shake my head. "It's really, really early days."

Fynn shrugs. "I think the key is just to stay open to it. Don't rush, but don't be too guarded that you miss who you're supposed to be with. I could quite easily have missed my opportunity to get to know Luce if someone hadn't given me the same advice."

"Thanks, Fynn."

"Do be careful with Andy, though. He's a good guy really, but a bit of a player. I'm not saying he would be with the right girl. I just don't want to see you get hurt again."

Fynn's words ring in my ears as Andy walks me to the door at the end of the night. Not only had I survived our date, it'd been easier than I'd thought once the nerves gave way. How ridiculous to think you could feel like a teenager with a crush again in your thirties. The butterflies feel as good as I remember, if not better for having lived without them for so long.

"What you thinking?" Andy asks as I turn to him by the front door.

"How content I feel tonight." I play with a strand of my hair. "I've had a really good night, so thank you."

"Do I sense a 'but' coming on?"

"But, rumour has it you're a bit of a player? I just don't want to put myself into a situation where I get hurt is all."

"I have been a player, I admit." He holds his hands up, palms forward. "Doesn't mean I will be when I meet the right girl. Just haven't been lucky enough yet." His eyes don't falter throughout his response. Not once does he look away.

"Fynn said something along those lines." I sigh. "I like you, Andy, and it feels good." I glance at him through the darkness.

"Well, Emma Millar, the feeling's mutual."

The next day I walk down the hill to where Andy's hammering fence posts into the ground. I'd asked my father this morning if he had any work for him on the farm and it had moved so fast that Andy had begun work straight away. However, now is the first I'd laid eyes on him, having spent the morning in one of the barns with the animals, feeding and mucking out.

"I know you. You're the scary farm owner's daughter. Have you come to discipline me for not working hard enough?" He smirks. "Do with me what you will." He holds out his arms in front of him as if I might shackle him as a punishment.

"Ha-ha-ha. Dream on," I say.

He makes my head spin as I can't help but notice his body, underneath his once-white, sweaty V-neck T-shirt.

"Here." I pass him a cold bottle of water. "I should probably just pour this over your head. You know, cool you off a little."

"Ah, but if you did I would be forced to retaliate and then we'd definitely be having some sort of wet T-shirt competition." He removes the top from the bottle and moves towards me.

"Don't you dare," I warn, realising I'm also wearing white. "You should stay back anyway, because I've been on mucking-out duties all morning in a hot, stinky barn."

"I can smell you from here." Andy fans in front of his nose.

"Hey." I play punch his shoulder, "You don't smell so good yourself."

With that, Andy flings an arm around me and rubs his sweaty body up against mine.

"Urgh, you're gross." I laugh uncontrollably and push against him in protest.

"It's endearing, admit it?"

"It's something, I'll give you that." I pause, basking in the sunshine as I rest on the fence beside him. "So, about tonight, can I know something about what we're doing?"

He shakes his head.

"Just a brief idea?"

"I plan on showering and picking you up at seven p.m., casual dress."

"I'm pleased you're going to shower." I continue our teasing. "But is that all I get?"

"For now." He flashes me one of his sexy smiles and I have to bite my lip.

"Fine, I'll see you at seven p.m." I slump my shoulders for effect and frown, but he's unmoved.

The rest of the day passes in a bit of a haze until it's

time to get ready. I've been unable to concentrate all day. Now in the shower is no different. I wash my hair twice, once almost accidentally with hair removal cream, which could have been a disaster. After thinking a little too hard about Andy's sexy smile, or the curve of his bicep when he grabbed me, I turn the cold water on myself before getting dry. *Emma Millar.*

The idea of a date alone with Andy sends my insides into a contorted mess. After umming and ahing over what to wear, I decided on my favourite cropped denim trousers, a white off-the-shoulder summer top and a pair of brown Birkenstock sandals. I grab a jacket, just in case, and push a pair of sunglasses on my freshly blow-dried hair, hoping this is what he meant by casual dress. Leaving my bedroom, I hear my mother speaking to someone in the kitchen.

"Emma dear, Andrew's here," she calls out.

Mum always uses people's full names. There are no abbreviations, ever. One of the many quirks I love about her.

Cantering down the stairs into the kitchen, I see my mum taking a roast chicken from the oven. The smell makes my mouth water and my stomach groan with hunger. I hope I'm correct in presuming Andy's plans involve food.

"Hey." I beam at him from the doorway, relieved that his shorts, black T-shirt and trainers combination means I'm dressed appropriately.

"Hey you," he greets me in return.

"Bye, Mum." I kiss her cheek before following

Andy out to his Jeep.

"Hope you're hungry?" he says, noticing me spy the picnic hamper in the back seat.

"Starving."

As the engine roars to life, the radio kicks in playing my favourite Ed Sheeran song and I relax into my seat. We haven't driven far before we pull into one of the back entrances to the estate.

"We have to walk from here, I'm afraid," he announces, gathering up the things from the back of the Jeep. He opens my door on his way round and I step out, letting him lead the way.

The heat from the day is fading fast, but the evening still has a pleasant warmth about it. I hear the trickle of water as we near the river and the birds are chirping and dancing around above our heads. As the trees clear, I see in the background an amazing view of the south side of the house, dominating the skyline. Andy lays out the picnic blanket not far from the river's edge and I sit down beside him. He opens up the basket and produces a bottle of fizz. The cork makes a confident pop sound before retiring on the grass.

"This is beautiful. I've never been to this spot before. How'd you find it?" I ask as Andy passes me a plastic champagne flute.

"With a little help from a friend. I told him I wanted to impress this really great girl and well …"

"I'm impressed," I admit.

"Cheers." He raises his glass to mine.

"Cheers."

"I hope these are all foods you like?"

Looking down I see many of my favourite foods, in a delicious-looking spread. The bread's still warm and its aroma wafts under my nose, mixed with the smell of sweet strawberries and rich chocolate brownies. Undoubtedly, Andy's had help with more than just the location.

After our feast, I munch on the drunk raspberry from the bottom of my now empty glass of fizz. The alcohol as per usual has gone straight to my head and I'm grateful for the fuzzy feeling I'm left with.

"So, Emma, Truth, or Dare?" He leans back onto his elbows.

"Really, you want to play Truth, or Dare? Is it the nineties?" I snigger.

"Dude, we were raised in the nineties," he says.

"True, *dude*! Well, go on then, Truth." My heart's in my mouth. I've no idea what he might ask. Neither do I have any idea what questions, or dares for that matter, I could ask him that wouldn't make me sound lame. Like, 'What's your favourite colour?'

"What's the first thing that attracts you to a guy, physically speaking?" he asks.

I relax a little, not hesitating in my response. "His eyes."

"Interesting. Any particular reason why?"

"I'm pretty sure that's two questions, but I'll answer you." I pretend to reprimand him. "I think you can tell a lot about a person from their eyes. How sincere and honest they are. Whether someone makes eye contact with you when speaking says a lot about them. Also eyes can be incredibly sexy."

"Noted." He pushes his sunglasses to the top of his head and his eyes don't leave mine.

"Truth, or dare?" I ask, still trying to hide the smile on my face.

Andy thinks for a moment before answering. "Truth."

"What would a girl have to have to change your playboy ways?" I freeze. Clearly the prosecco effect is making me far braver than I feel.

"Good question." He pauses, but I'm relieved he doesn't seem offended. "There was a girl once. We were together for three years, engaged for one."

Surprised by his revelation, I wait for him to go on.

"As the wedding plans got underway we started to argue and were spending less time together. In the end we both just realised it wasn't working, so we called off the wedding and went our separate ways."

"That must have been tough?" I sympathise.

"It was hard, but was the right thing to do for us both."

"I guess at least you figured it out in time."

"There is that." He pours the remains of the bottle into my glass. "So in answer to your question, I suppose she would have to be someone I can see myself settling down with—probably someone who's five foot nine, with brown hair, a cute nose, killer ass, and goes by the name, Emma."

"Ha-ha-ha." I take a sip of my drink.

"Truth, or dare, Miss Millar?"

It's weird hearing Andy call me that. Chris is normally the only one who refers to me as 'Miss Millar'.

"Truth?" My head pulls back and my shoulders push forwards, wishing I could shake the odd feeling in the pit of my stomach.

Andy's humming, unreadable, leaning back relaxing on his elbows.

"Worst Fear?" is his next question.

I think of spiders or heights, the usual suspects, but what comes to my mind isn't the obvious. "History repeating itself." I let out a shallow sigh and stare ahead of me.

"I didn't mean to upset you." He sits forward.

"You didn't, sorry. I'm being too deep for a second date. I should have just said spiders or something …"

"Well, technically it's our third date if we're counting the ball and it's not like we're strangers. His body's closer to mine now. "What do you mean by history repeating itself, your marriage ending?"

Andy doesn't know the whole story. Not many people knew about the baby. I take a sip of my drink.

"I fell pregnant not long after Matt and I started dating." I look up at the sky as the sun makes its final descent of the day. When I look back at him he's trying to hide his shock, but his slightly dazed expression means he's only half succeeding.

"What happened?"

"We told our families, no one else, and hastily got engaged. I'd always wanted to do things the 'right way round', not that I'm sure anybody cares which way round things are done these days, but I did … do. In a flash, everything was booked and organised: the church, the reception venue, the dress, suits, everything. Two weeks before the wedding, I had a miscarriage. I was twelve weeks pregnant at the time."

He shakes his head and I fear I've shared too much.

"But you still got married, why?"

"I thought that's what I wanted, and it was at the time. Blinded by love, youth, or a bit of both, I suppose. Truth is, I just couldn't bear to lose anything else." I pause. "So when I say I'm scared of history repeating itself, I'm scared of making those mistakes all over again and being back here. Recovering from heartbreak, alone."

Andy breaks eye contact.

"I don't mean that quite how it came out. Being here with you is really nice." I stroke his arm. "When you marry the wrong person the first time around, it makes you worry that you might make the same mistake again. I don't think I could survive this twice, that's all."

"It must have been tough losing a baby and all the pressure of the wedding," he says, his eyebrows pulling down.

"It was confusing mostly. I was pretty up and down emotionally back then. Perhaps not really the best time to decide the rest of your life. Hindsight's a wonderful thing, though, right?" I mock myself. "I always thought I'd be married for a couple of years before having a baby, so it took me the whole of my first trimester to process everything. Matt bought a ring and proposed, but I was too morning sick to enjoy that major milestone in life. About a week before my first scan, I started to feel excited about the baby, the wedding, all of it. It became real all of a sudden, instead of this odd dream I'd felt trapped inside for weeks. During the scan, they couldn't find a heartbeat. They called it a 'missed miscarriage'."

He's holding me now and my cheeks feel wet from tears I'm unwillingly crying.

"What happened after that?"

"They said the options were to wait and see if things started 'naturally', or have surgery to remove the pregnancy. The doctor recommended the latter, especially with the wedding so close."

"I'm so sorry, Em."

"I'm fine." I wipe my face with the back of my hand. "Sorry for the overshare."

"Don't be. Do you think you would have gotten married if you hadn't fallen pregnant?"

"Honestly, I don't know. I thought I was in love, but sometimes that's just not enough. Anyway, Truth, or Dare?"

"Wow, you changed that conversation like a pro." He looks at me as if he isn't sure I'm okay, but thankfully doesn't press the subject. "Dare."

I put my head in my hands. “No! I was dreading you saying that. I literally have nothing.”

“I have a dare you could use.” He smirks.

“Go on.” I narrow my eyes.

“You could dare me to kiss you?” He leans towards me so his face is inches from mine. As I breathe in the smell of his cologne, our previous conversation becomes a distant memory.

“Do you want to kiss me?” I whisper into the silence between us, our eyes firmly locked on each other.

“I do,” is all he mutters in return.

“I dare you … to kiss me.”

With that he lifts my chin, placing his soft warm lips on mine, where he lingers a while. We part and I leave my eyes closed for a few seconds.

“Truth, or Dare?” he utters.

“Dare.” I open my eyes to find him still inches away from my lips.

“Kiss me again.”

I lean in, my body falling onto his. We kiss until the night gets darker and the sky fills with stars above us. The sound of night bugs and water trickling downstream fills the air. There’s a cool breeze after the heat of the daytime, but I don’t feel the chill wrapped in Andy’s strong arms. A quiet contentment washes over me and, for the first time, my fears fade into the background as I allow myself to dream that perhaps a happier ending may exist after all.

Chapter 8

Something clatters on the floor beside me and I look up from my daydream to see waiters clearing dessert plates away in unison. It's one week since our last date and Andy and I are sitting at a long table in the dining room at Wincastle. Earlier in the week, Chris had invited us to join him for a dinner party hosted by his parents. Andy's been working away all week, so I've only spoken to him on the phone and I still feel a little vulnerable after sharing so much with him sitting by the river. Since stirring up all those old emotions, I've been thinking about the summer when 'it' happened, a lot.

A waitress offers me more wine.

"No, thank you." I hold my hand over my glass. I'm working tomorrow, so I'm the DD this evening—designated driver."

"Welcome back."

I turn my attention back to him.

"You drifted off into your own world there. Was the chocolate torte that good?"

"You know me and chocolate." I wink.

I'm pleased I don't need to explain where my mind was just now, or, as attentive as he's been during dinner, how my attention keeps being drawn to the table opposite. Chris is beside the beautiful redhead from the ball, who's wearing a tight white cocktail dress, with wavy loose hair against her pale complexion and perfect apricot lips which suit her. I'm not sure what she's doing at Wincastle this time, but I think Chris is hiding something. In fact, I'm sure of it. Even more so, given every time he catches my eye, he immediately looks away.

"Who's the woman next to Chris?" I ask Andy, leaning forward.

"Charlotte Harrington."

I wait, holding his eye contact. I need more than her name, and from the look on his face, he realises it.

"I think she's an old family friend," he says, his brows pulling together, playing dumb.

"Really?"

"Em, this isn't my place. Let me get you another …"

"Andy!"

He knocks back his wine before turning towards me. "I told him to tell you weeks ago."

"Tell me what?"

"Maybe this is a conversation you should be having with him."

I stand, my posture stiff, my muscles rigid. "Andy, just …"

"She's Chris's fiancée."

I inhale sharply, and for the first time this evening Chris meets my gaze with trepidation in his eyes. I notice him whisper something to Charlotte before standing up as I walk out.

Reaching the top of the grand staircase, I practically burst through a set of doors and into the gallery, where I pace up and down, heat flushing through my body.

"Emma, let me explain …"

"You're engaged?"

Chris is standing still, his hands spread out in front of him as if taming a wild animal.

"Yes."

"That's what you'd gone to tell Colin last week, before I arrived?"

"Yes."

"Who is she?"

"Her name is Charlotte."

"I know her name, Chris." I draw in slow steady breaths. "Why didn't you tell me you're engaged?"

"I wanted to—I was going to." His voice wavers.

I send him a long, pained look. "Do you even know her a little?" I clench my teeth together.

"I've known Charlotte and her parents for a few years. Mostly through functions. She's been away at uni."

"Doesn't sound to me as if you know her very well, but you're considering spending the rest of your life with her?" The floorboards creak as I slowly pace them.

"We've been spending some time together and it's

just progressed from there. I couldn't exactly tell you I'm getting married when you came home so heartbroken, could I?"

"And since? You couldn't tell me in the time we've been spending together since, now that I'm feeling stronger? I thought we were closer than this."

"I'm sorry I didn't find the time to tell you." He loosens his tie. "The longer I left it, the more I've been dreading it."

"So you thought it was easier to keep it from me and let me find out from everyone else? I'm your oldest friend and when I asked you about your love life you didn't even mention seeing anyone. Not a word. You're engaged, Chris!"

"Yes!" he shouts back, gripping his hair, before running his hand down his face.

I rub at the middle of my forehead; there's a burning sensation in my chest. "Do you love her?"

"I do … It took me by surprise when I fell for her, Em. I wasn't looking to get involved with anyone, but something with us just clicked. Plus, she's rich in her own right, so she's not after me for my money." He laughs, trying to make light of some part of this. "Please accept my apology for not telling you sooner. I genuinely was trying to protect you and I knew you'd think I was rushing into something, but I'm not."

I stand still, as though I'm cast out of stone.

"Emma, say something."

"… You're the person I trust most in the world, I just hate feeling as though I've been lied to, that's all, but that's my issue, not yours, so I'm sorry for overreacting."

"I know. I wouldn't like it if you kept something like this from me either. I'm truly sorry." He moves towards me with his arms open and I walk into them.

"Are you happy for me?"

"Of course I'm happy for you," I say, but a huge part of me isn't sure I mean it.

Chapter 9

A month's passed since the dinner party, where the next morning Chris left for France on holiday with Charlotte and her parents. Even now, sitting crossed-legged on the dark brown carpet of my new one-bed haven, surrounded by boxes, I'm not sure how to feel about it, but try not to let it dampen my spirits. This morning, I collected my keys from the letting agents and I'm so excited to have my own home once more.

The lounge is small, running directly into the kitchen, which is also small. There are open timber stairs in the back of the room, and an old brick fireplace, next to which stands the flat screen television that my parents gave me, on a light wooden stand. Tomorrow, Andy's collecting the dark blue three-seater Ikea sofa, which I'd bought second-hand online. It will clash with the existing green floral-print fusty-smelling curtains, but they are purposeful until I can afford to change them.

The house has a general fusty smell, as if no windows have been open in months, if not years. The previous tenant was an elderly lady, who at the grand age of ninety-four, sadly passed away in her sleep. Mrs Ellison, a retired primary school head teacher, rented the small cottage with her late husband, Councillor Ellison, who passed away fifteen years before her. They were a lovely couple and I remember them both fondly. Their son wanted her to move down south to live with him in Dorset after his father died. 'I won't leave my Cyril,' she would tell me when I'd bump into her in the village doing a bit of shopping. Cyril is buried in the local cemetery, where she now joins him. It gives me goosebumps every time I think about their true love and dedication to one another. If not only for the memories of others who had lived here, I already feel quite attached to this house.

The property is one of many owned by the estate as part of their investment portfolio, and at first Sir Richard suggested that I live here rent-free, but I didn't feel comfortable with such a charitable gesture. Realising I wouldn't be moved on the issue, he reluctantly set a price, though it's far lower than he would have charged anyone else, I'm sure. I'm grateful, though, for the help until I'm back on my feet. Living back with my parents has been just what I needed. Now, though, I'm pleased to be getting my independence back. What with my new job and things between Andy and me going so well, it's a fresh start. My life is finally getting back on track.

I'm still riffling through boxes when Andy arrives back with the Chinese.

"Don't suppose you found the glasses?" He gives

me his broadest smile, while holding up a bottle. "To toast the new digs with."

As I wrap my arms around his neck, he kisses me and I hold my breath, melting. It's strange how quickly I'm falling for him. Never did I imagine being this happy or meeting someone who makes me feel special, in the many ways he does.

"Thank you. We may have to use these mugs as I seem to have hidden glasses from myself." I hold up two mismatched mugs in one hand and gesture around the room at the mess with the other. "Good news is I did find the forks and plates. They're in the kitchen on the side."

I watch as he turns an empty box upside down, placing a pillow on the floor. He grabs me by the hand, taking me by surprise and spinning me around towards the makeshift table.

"Your chair, my lady."

I take my seat on the pillow and a familiar surge of contentment runs through my body. It's the simple things he does which make me happy. Like this makeshift box table and the way he manages to make everything feel so romantic. If I had to write a list of my favourite traits of his, thoughtful and kind are up near the top. Closely followed by his ridiculous good looks. I would describe him as a dark-haired Ryan Gosling, with the physique to match. And judging by how many women look at him when we're out together, I'm not the only one who thinks it.

I've finished shredding the duck for our starter

when he returns from the kitchen.

"Why are you staring at me like that?"

"Because you're amazing and you make me smile. Plus you're fit, too, which is an added bonus."

He doesn't say anything in return, he just leans over the table and kisses me intently, leaving me breathless, my skin flushing. If I hadn't been so hungry, I may have changed my mind about eating altogether following that kiss. However, we're taking things slow in that department. He releases me and sits back down smiling to himself, knowing precisely the effect he has on me and I doubt there's a man alive who doesn't relish that.

Our starter is the best duck I've tasted in a long time. It's from a little Chinese takeaway which has recently opened in the village. I make a mental note to avoid getting into the habit of eating takeaway too often. What with my shifts and living in my new place it will be too tempting to swing past the Chinese on the way home, or my favourite chip shop in the village, which we seem to have done a fair bit of late.

He disappears into the kitchen to fetch our main courses and I hear the dull sound of my phone vibrating somewhere. Moving aside bits of bubble wrap and boxes, I stumble upon it as it rings off.

"What's up?" he asks as he returns.

"I've missed a call from Jo at work. I think she's on nights tonight. I hope she's not trying to get me to cover someone's shift."

"Probably best you missed it then," he says with a wink.

"I'd happily help Jo out. I'm going to miss her when she goes back to live in Cornwall in a few months."

"Why did you two lose contact?"

"I guess it was a distance thing. We're friends on Facebook, but we just didn't meet up while I was living away. We used to have such a laugh when we were student nurses. Especially on placements, when we were lucky enough to get assigned to the same ward at the hospital. A&E was one of the places we worked together and I remember us both knowing it was where we wanted to get a job once we qualified."

"Yeah, shame you two've reconnected just before she's leaving. On the plus side, cheap holidays in Cornwall for the summer." He pours me some wine.

Laughing, I open up the container set in front of me, savouring the sweet smell as I spoon some of the pork and beansprouts onto my plate. Trust Andy to have a silver lining.

"To the future, Miss Millar," he says.

"The Future."

We clink mugs and I take a sip. It's felt a long time coming, but the future seems as though it's something to look forward to. As I look around my bare living room of possibilities, I know this is a new beginning. A blank canvas. I can do whatever I want with it and be whoever I want to be here. It will be a happy place and somewhere where I can make some new memories.

"Have you heard from Chris?" Andy asks, disturbing my sense of peace momentarily.

"No. I wasn't expecting to while he's on holiday." I fork bits of rice around my plate. The truth is, I'm still upset Chris didn't tell me he's engaged, Andy knows that, but at least we parted friends. It even crossed my mind that he may be married already. A shotgun wedding in France, perhaps. Then I remember if nothing else, he wouldn't do that to his parents.

I continue my silence because I don't want to talk about it. Abandoning the conversation, he clears the plates.

To be less than happy for him makes me a hypocrite, because he'd protested about my marriage to Matt and I hadn't listened. Deep down, I feel as though he's making a mistake. I just wish he'd see that for himself and get to know her before rushing ahead with wedding plans. If Chris's grandfather were still alive, he would have been the first to warn against rushing into marriage with someone you barely know. His own marriage to Granny had been a whirlwind romance, and once the honeymoon phase was over, he'd spent a lifetime suffering the consequences of that decision.

My thoughts are interrupted by my phone vibrating in my hand. It's Jo again. If it were anyone else from work, I wouldn't answer, but I can't ignore her.

"Hey you, I thought you're on nights?"

"I am … I …" The line goes quiet for too long before Jo speaks again. "An RTA came in tonight and the driver wasn't carrying any ID … Emma, I recognise him." Jo pauses for longer this time. "It's your friend, Chris." The room circles around me as I scramble to my feet, grasping at the white wall by the front door for support. I bend forward, inhaling and exhaling, trying to catch my breath.

"How is he?" I eventually ask, bringing my thoughts back into focus.

"He's tubed and unconscious, but not on a ventilator. They're taking him to CT now."

"Have you told his family?" I ask.

"His parents are registered as his next of kin, but I haven't been able to contact them. They might send the police out."

"No!" I shout and Andy rushes beside me. "I'll tell them, don't let them send the police, Jo, please." The wall on which I'm leaning is cold against my bare arm. The skin on my entire body seems to tighten as I imagine the police turning up at the estate. "Jo, look after him until I get there, please," I plead.

"Of course."

With that, I hang up.

Andy's talking to me, but I can't hear him. The air catches in my throat, making it hard to breathe as I fumble at the door handle. Barefoot, I stand on the path and feel as though I might be sick. Chris is hurt, maybe badly.

"Emma!" he shouts and I jolt to my senses. "What's happened?" He's grasping the top of my arms tightly and I realise I must look as if I'm going to pass out.

"Chris has been in a car accident."

"Is it serious?" he asks.

"I don't know. I need to go and tell Elizabeth. Lucy's away, so is Sir Richard." I cover my face with my hands and feel him scoop me into his arms.

"Come on, we need to go, get your shoes and I'll drive you. We can try and reach Luce on the way."

He didn't say it will be fine. He hasn't said anything, which worries me because he's normally big on reassurance. Andy lived through the aftermath of Stephens's death, too. He may not have been local when it happened, but he attended the funeral of the friend he'd grown up with. No doubt, it was on his mind that this wouldn't be fine. That Chris wouldn't be fine.

I dial Lucy's phone from the car.

"No luck?"

"Voicemail." I massage my temple.

"She'll call back," he says, concentrating on the windy roads. I've never known Andy to drive so carefully.

The journey feels as though it's taking far longer than normal and my mind is unable to suppress old memories. Memories of the time when I found Chris in the treehouse after Stephens's death. He'd been missing for hours and Lucy had pleaded with me to look for him. I'd known precisely where to find him.

As I climb the steps of the treehouse, I'm not sure what I'm going to say to him. He's lying on the floor, motionless, staring up at the ceiling. I move alongside him and edge my fingertips towards his hand on the ground between us. We lie there a long while without speaking, just holding hands and staring at the craggy treehouse roof.

Stephen's dead. There are no words for that. If I'm struggling this much with the loss of my surrogate brother figure, then I'm not sure how Chris, his own flesh and blood, will get through this.

"Mum's locked herself in her room," he eventually says. "She won't talk to anyone, hasn't even cried. Well, at least, not in front of us."

"I can't imagine how you must be feeling right now, how you must all feel." I sit up, looking down at Chris, who doesn't make eye contact. "What can I do? Tell me what I can do?" Tears form in my eyes and drip, one by one, onto his jumper below.

"I don't know, Em. You can't fix this. Nothing's ever going to be the same." He clenches his jaw tight. "I miss him so much already," he blurts out, sobs raging from him as he cries in a way I've never witnessed.

"I miss him too." I cover his body with mine and we lie, awash in each other's tears.

I wipe my cheek as I wait in the lounge for the housekeeper to fetch Elizabeth, who appears moments later in her robe and slippers.

"Emma, whatever is the matter?" she asks, entering

the room, looking as bewildered as I feel.

"Elizabeth, I …" I know the words about to leave my lips will break her heart or what remains of it.

"It's Chris, he's been hurt in an accident. A car accident."

Her legs buckle.

I step forward to catch her and ease her into the armchair. "He's in good hands. The team I work with are fantastic. My friend Jo's looking after him." I'm trying to reassure myself as much as her. The truth is, the team I work with are fantastic, but I don't know the extent of his injuries and it scares me. Too many times I've looked after car accident victims who don't survive. The perils of being a nurse; you always know that bit too much. "We need to go to the hospital," I say, feeling the panic rising within me.

"Yes." She stands. "I need to get dressed. Richard and Lucy are away, so I was having an early night, you see." Her face is pasty-white and impassive, which matches her tone.

"Don't worry, I'll help you."

Andy pulls up outside the entrance to A&E and I climb out of the car, offering my arm to Elizabeth for support as she does the same. There's a familiar robotic clunk as the automatic door to the department drones open to a busy-as-usual waiting room. We queue at the reception, hearing the radio humming in the background and I can smell a multifarious mix of blood, sweat, and alcohol in the air. The man in front of us is wearing just one shoe and hopping on his right foot. Another woman is holding a crying baby. The sign on the desk signals that the waiting time is three hours, so I know triage must be busy.

"Emma." The brunette woman wearing a blue spotty blouse shouts to me from behind the reception desk.

"Amanda, where's Jo?" I ask in haste.

"She told me to take you through to the relatives' room."

Immediately suspecting the worst, I feel as if my legs might give way. Why would Jo need us to go into the relatives' room and not straight in to see him? My mind is racing at the thought it must be bad news. Poor Elizabeth, this will kill her for sure.

Only now, as I sit next to her on the sofa do I notice the details of the room I've been in hundreds of times as a nurse, never as a relative. There are no windows, which makes it feel warm and claustrophobic, and the lighting is harsh and bright, like most of the hospital strip lighting. A dark wooden coffee table sits in the centre of the room with several tea rings engrained in the surface. The sofa and two chairs are grey—*such a sombre colour.* Elizabeth reaches for my hand and I squeeze it.

Why is it taking so long? Where's Jo? I fiddle with my bracelet, fighting the urge to go out and find him myself, though I'm not ready to have the worst confirmed just yet. I can't leave Elizabeth, either, who is still gripping my hand, to the point that it feels numb. I look down and see a small photo in her other hand. Noticing me looking, she shows it to me. It's a picture of Chris and Stephen as boys sitting on my dad's tractor at the farm.

"I remember that summer," she whispers. "I barely saw the boys because they were at the farm from dawn until dusk helping your father."

I close my eyes and breathe in the memory. When I open them, it's as if I'm staring into the face of a more familiar person. Her eyes are no longer those of a cold stranger. There's warmth and sorrow in the way she's looking at me, something I haven't seen in her eyes for a long time.

"I know I've been different … since he passed away. It's a loss beyond words losing a child, but to lose two children … I'm not sure I can bear that."

"We're not going to lose him." I wrap my arms around my once motherlike figure and for the first time in years, she cries, while I hold her.

Moments pass and the door opens. In walks Jo, followed by the Lead Trauma Consultant, Dr Andrews. I feel the insides of my cheeks stinging as bile rises from my stomach and take several deep breaths through my nose to try to stay calm. *Look at Jo,* I tell myself, she won't be able to hide it from you. You know her too well. If she can look at you, he's alive, if she can't … he's dead.

"Mrs Golding, Emma." The consultant's tone is gentle.

I look up slowly at my friend and, to my relief, Jo eyes meet mine. I breathe out, tipping back my head.

"The good news is that your son has regained consciousness and has been able to tell us who and where he is."

My whole body relaxes so quickly I think I might faint. Elizabeth lets out a loud gasp of relief and turns to hug me.

"I told you he'd be fine," I say, even though not one part of me had believed it.

"Now he's still fairly groggy, but his initial head CT and X-rays are all clear. He does have a concussion, facial lacerations and bruising to his ribs, but by some kind of miracle, nothing is broken. He's very, very lucky indeed." The consultant touches my arm as he leaves the room.

"Thank you." I return the gesture.

"We've moved him into a side room on the observation ward. I'll take you there now." Jo hugs me tightly.

"Thank you." I grab her hand when she releases me.

As Jo leads us to him, a surge of strange emotions washes over me. In the past four weeks, I've boxed up and buried my feelings, the feelings that scare me. It started when I saw Chris across the table with Charlotte at the dinner party and I'd had the urge to drag her away from him by her hair. Finding out he's engaged to her made the ache in my heart return and I can't believe how vulnerable it's left me. Only now, after thinking I might have lost him, do I allow myself to feel what I've been desperately trying to ignore.

I'm in love with Chris and no amount of suppression or denial is going to change that.

Chapter 10

"Chris, can you hear me?" Jo shines the light in his right eye, then his left.

"Yeah." He moves his head and strains to open his eyes.

"It's just the effect of the morphine," Jo tells Elizabeth, to explain his grogginess.

"Chris, I'm just going to shine my torch in your eye again, okay?"

"Mum," he says in a hoarse voice.

"Darling, I'm here." She takes his hand, and as Jo's light recedes, he tries to open his eyes fully.

"You're doing great, Chris," Jo reassures him, stepping back.

"Sorry," he says, and when he tries to swallow, a crease forms on his brow.

"For what, darling?"

"Scaring you."

"You're safe, that's all that matters." She leans into him on the bed and he grimaces.

"Sorry." She eases back, stroking his cheek tenderly around his cuts.

Chris flinches, though, this time I'm not sure

whether it's due to pain or if he's trying to register his mother's unexpected affection.

"They look worse than they feel, Mum," he croaks. "Can I have a drink, please?" he says, opening and closing his dry lips.

I move towards the jug on the cabinet. "Here." I pass him the plastic cup and hover.

"I need to phone your father. Emma, please will you stay with him while I make some telephone calls?"

"Of course."

"I'll be straight back," she says.

The room's quieter now there are fewer bodies in it.

"Are you too warm?" I ask, noticing Chris looking at the window.

"I could do with some air, if that's okay?" He coughs, grabbing his side with a moan.

"Is that better?" I push the window as far as it will go and the curtain begins swaying idly in the breeze.

"Much, thank you. Now if you could just use your magic nurse's wand to stop my ribs from hurting this much, please."

"I wish I could." I resume my place by the locker, nearest the door.

"I'm …" We say in unison. He winces again and I can almost feel his pain too.

"I, I'm so sorry for upsetting you before I left, Emma." Unable to project his voice, he massages his throat.

"No, I'm sorry. I hate it when we fight, and then

you nearly killed yourself." Tears roll down my cheeks. "I can't lose you too, Chris."

He reaches forward, grabbing my hand, the pain etched in lines on his forehead. "Hey, you can't get rid of me that easily."

I lean over and hug him as gently as I can, but he still stiffens in my arms.

"Sorry, did I hurt you?"

"A little. If this is what bruised ribs feel like, I never want to experience broken ones. Could you pass me some more water, please? My throat is so dry."

Refilling his cup, I hand it back to him. "Here," I say, dragging my chair closer to his bed, making vibrations on the floor. "Do you remember much about what happened in the accident?"

He rests his head back on the pillow, staring up at the ceiling tiles above his head. "I was on the back road about twenty minutes from home. I'd been driving for a while when the fuel light came on and when I checked for my wallet at the services, I didn't have it. I remembered Charlotte putting it in her handbag on the flight home, so I phoned her to check she still had it."

"You were on your phone," I scold.

"I was using Bluetooth and she didn't answer, so I left a voicemail," he says.

My shoulders relax.

"After a mile or so more I saw something in the road. I think a stag. I tried to swerve, but it happened so quickly. I must have clipped a tree or something because after that all I remember is waking up here."

My hands are in a praying position in front of my lips and I'm shaking my head.

"Stephen had only been twenty minutes from home when he crashed, Em. That's how close he was, all those years ago."

"You're safe now." I instinctively take his hand and kiss it softly.

He uses his free hand to stroke my face.

"A good thing Charlotte wasn't with you," I say, sitting back, releasing his hand. "Where is she now?"

"She had to be in London this week for work. I don't think she knows about the accident. I should call her."

"I can do that," I offer.

"Thank you." He touches my hand and my skin prickles.

"Your father's on his way home, he'll be here in the morning. I still haven't managed to reach your sister, though," Elizabeth says, now back in the room.

"It's late, Mum. You should go home to bed." He turns to me. "Please will you take Mum home?"

"Of course." I nod. Andy's outside."

"No, I would rather stay, Christopher."

I stroke her arm. "Why don't I stay? Andy can take you home and then you can come back in the morning after a good night's sleep."

Elizabeth plays with the top button of her cardigan. "Will you be okay?" she asks as she leans over and kisses her son's forehead.

"I'll be fine, Mum. Don't worry." He blows her a kiss.

I wonder how strange this is for him, seeing his mum with her guard down. After losing Stephen, the happy, loving, fun-filled house that existed in his childhood disappeared overnight, replaced with a dark cloud of depression and sadness that never really lifted. It hadn't been an easy time to be around the family, nonetheless I sat with Elizabeth for hours so she wasn't alone in her grief. One day she woke up and pretended nothing had happened. She didn't cry, but then she no longer laughed either. No one was allowed past her impenetrable shield, not even her own husband, or children. It was as though Stephen's death took away her soul.

"You okay?" I ask Chris, who's slipped down the bed and looks uncomfortable.

"I need to sit higher, but I'm too sore to move myself," he says.

"I'm not surprised. Let me help you." I rest one knee on the bed, leaning into him so our shoulders touch and use my body as a lever to lift him forwards. With my free hand, I rearrange his pillows and manoeuvre him into a better position. Our eyes lock as I lower him back down.

"Thank you, nurse."

You're welcome, patient." I smile and look away, resisting the urge to stare into his eyes for longer.

He watches me closely as I fold the top of the sheet in a neat line down over the pale green blanket.

"Am I tidy now, Sister Millar?"

"You'll do."

I notice him drifting off to sleep, so I sit beside him and let him rest.

"Sorry, I must have dozed off again," he says upon waking half an hour or so later.

"It's good for you to rest. The body heals when we sleep. Can I do anything?"

"You could tell me what I've missed in your world lately, to distract me from the pain?" he says.

"I'm renting the Ellisons' old cottage. I was unpacking when I heard about your accident."

"I'm sorry I interrupted you moving in."

"You're more important than moving house, Chris. It'll keep."

"The place is perfect for you. I'm pleased my father thought to offer you it."

"It really is." I beam. "Though he's barely charging me any rent, which I feel guilty for."

"He'd let you live there rent free and you know it."

"He tried, but I couldn't accept."

"That doesn't surprise me." He pauses. "How are things with you and Andy?"

"Okay."

"Is that all I get?"

He watches me intently as I bounce my knees. "What do you want me to say?"

"Is it serious between the two of you?"

I roll my shoulders forward, looking at him. "He says he's in love with me."

"Love? He said that?" His voice squeaks like an adolescent boy and he clears his throat, nursing his side.

"He said it to me a couple of days ago."

"So soon?" he asks, but it's really more of a statement than a question. "Did you say it back?"

"I didn't." I shuffle in my seat.

He lifts his eyebrows.

"What?" I ask.

"Nothing."

"Oh, come off it, it's never nothing when you make that face."

Chris is trying to pick his words carefully. "I just think it's a bit soon for him to be telling you that."

"A bit soon? Are we really gonna go there?"

"Sorry. I'm just being …"

"Over-protective—I know." I nod.

"How about you and Charlotte?" *I hate that name.*

Chris rolls his shoulders forward, much in the same way I had. "I don't really know what to say." He steals a sideways look at me.

"The truth is always a good place to start."

"… We've set a date for the wedding."

The words hang mid-air for what feels like several uncomfortable minutes. I lower my head and fall silent.

"Em, say something."

"Congratulations," I muster. "When's the happy day?" I hope I sounded more sincere than I feel.

"August. Two weeks after Lucy and Fynn's."

So many unsaid thoughts fill the void between us.

"Chris, I …"

He strains forward, his face contorted with pain, just as the door to the side room opens and Charlotte rushes in.

"I was so worried. I got your voicemail and tried calling you back. I waited, but when I didn't hear from you again I just got in my car." She exhales. "I was almost at the estate when your mother called me to tell me what happened. Are you all right?" she asks, kissing his face.

"Hey, hey, it's okay. I'm okay." Chris strokes her hair before looking over at me. Charlotte sits back as if noticing my presence for the first time, though I sense she's not as oblivious as she's appearing.

"Emma, hi. Sorry, I didn't notice you there. Lovely to see you again, though not in these particular circumstances, obviously."

"It's good to see you, too, Charlotte." I sound sincere, but feel myself flinch when she gives me a hug.

Chris coughs, arching his back, and clutches at his side.

"I'll get the nurse to get you something for the pain on my way out."

"You don't have to go," he says.

"You've got Charlotte here now, so there's no need

for me to stay. Besides, the nurses won't want two people here. Charlotte might get away with staying, but I know the rules, so I should go." I gather my bag. "I'll come back tomorrow. Try and get some rest," I order.

"I will."

"Lovely to see you, Charlotte," I say again, touching her arm.

"Thank you for looking after him until I got here."

I've been looking after him long before you got here. I give her a smile that wavers and turn to leave.

"Em." Chris commands my attention.

"Thanks for looking out for Mum tonight. It means a lot."

"Always."

Chapter 11

Mum walks into the kitchen to me opening and closing the cupboards with force.

"I wish whatever it is that's bothering you wasn't being taken out on my poor kitchen."

I stop for a second and notice her wholesome expression. In an instant, my mood softens as it always does when she's around.

"Sorry, Mum. I just can't find Dad's flask. I said I would make him some coffee."

She passes me, reaching up into the side cupboard where I'd just been looking and pulls down a silver metal flask.

"Here you go," she says without any hidden tone in her voice.

"Thank you," I say, feeling ridiculous for the fuss I've just been making.

"Is Christopher home?"

"Yes, he went home a few days ago."

"And he's fine?"

"As far as I know. I haven't seen him."

She fills the kettle, sets it to boil, and leans against

the sink in front of the window where a flicker of sunlight dances on top of her grey hair. "Are you going to tell me what the matter is?"

I let out a long-drawn-out sigh.

"Something to do with Chris? Andy? Am I to keep guessing?" she asks as she goes about spooning coffee and sugar into a Pyrex jug ready for pouring into the flask.

"It's both of them and neither of them." I flop onto the bench and lean my elbows on the table, holding my chin in the palms of my hands. She joins me and places a gentle hand on my wrist.

"I don't know how to explain it, Mum."

"Just say it how it comes out and let's see what we can make of it." Her tone is soothing.

"The other night when I was with Chris and Elizabeth at the hospital I felt part of it again."

"Part of what?"

"The family."

"Of course you're part of the family, as Chris and Lucy are part of ours."

"You know it's not been the same, not since Stephen died. Just for a short while it was as if we were all connected again for the first time in forever."

"And?"

"Then Charlotte turned up and I didn't know my place anymore. Charlotte's the fiancée, I'm just … his friend. I suppose it's how he must have felt when I met Matt, but I never realised until now. I wasn't around much when he was dating Gabby, so I've never really felt …"

"Pushed out?"

"Yes." I nod.

"It's understandable you wanting to be there for him, you've been through a lot together. Things will be different now that he has someone. I'm sure he still needs you in his life and you will always be part of the Goldings family, but you're not kids anymore, sweetheart." She rubs my back.

"I know," I say, folding my arms in front of me.

"Besides, you have Andy. Things are okay there, aren't they?"

"They're fine, why?" I couldn't bring myself to tell her the whole truth.

"You said it was both of them?"

"Did I? I'm just tired."

"Well, don't help Dad today, have a rest. He won't mind."

"I'll take him his coffee. I did promise after all."

She strokes my hair as she passes behind me to finish filling the flask.

I don't stay with Dad long, he's busy and I don't want to make small talk. Instead, I decide to feed the animals. Mum told me to rest, but I need a distraction and some space to think, which I can always rely on the farm for.

The day so far isn't too warm, nonetheless it's a beautiful summer's morning without a single cloud in the bright blue sky. Aside from the chickens, clucking and scatting around at my feet in the corn I'm absentmindedly scattering, it's peaceful.

Andy's a great guy, he makes me smile, and until this past week, I almost believed that I might fall for him. Chris's accident and his engagement to Charlotte has stirred up feelings inside me that I can't shake and I don't know how to deal with.

"Those chickens are going to think all their Christmases have come at once."

I jump, sending the feed hurtling to the floor.

"Sorry, I didn't mean to startle you." Andy leans in to kiss me.

"That's okay." I bend down to retrieve the bag as the chickens climb over one another to reach the ever-increasing pile of food.

"You okay?" he asks.

My desire right now is to flee, because the conversation I know I need to have with him isn't going to be easy. I move my lips, but no words come out. "Can we talk?" I eventually say.

"Sounds serious."

Andy takes a seat on a patch of grass where I join him. There's a silence at first. I can't bring myself to look him in the eye. Instead, I focus on his arm resting over his bent knee, playing with a strand of grass. My stomach feels as though it's rolling. He deserves better than my uncertainty.

"It's not you." I pull up a grass strand of my own and peel it. "I know it sounds like a cliché, but it really has more to do with me."

He waits for me to continue.

"There's just so much going on, you know, what with Chris's accident, the two weddings of the century, and my divorce." I waft the air with my hand.

His jawline's set as his head moves slowly up and down. "You breaking up with me?" There's an audible tremor in his tone and the look in his eyes almost pierces my soul.

"I don't know," I croak. "You and I, it took me by surprise." My head's moving from side to side. "I just …" I massage the bridge of my nose to fight the tears that are backing up. "I feel so confused right now. Maybe this is all too soon after all?"

Turning his body towards me, he cups my hands in his. "You know how I feel about you, Emma," he says as his somewhat broken confidence recuperates momentarily. "If you need time or space to figure this out, then okay."

I touch his face and he leans his warm stubbly cheek into the palm of my hand.

"I've been offered a job working on my friend's farm in Lincolnshire for the summer. I turned it down because I didn't want to leave you, but I think I'll go."

His face is blurry from the tears in my eyes. "I don't want you to go … I don't know what I want." I kneel in front of him, hot tears streaming down my increasingly splotchy face.

"Hey, don't cry." He wipes both of my cheeks with the bottom of his T-shirt. "This is exactly what I don't want for you. You've been through too much already this year."

I sink forward into his chest and smell his familiar comforting woodsy smell that I've come to know. He peels me off, gently lifting my chin, "I'm coming back." He strokes my cheek. "And when I do, if this is what you want, if I'm what you want, then okay. You need to figure that out." He kisses me swiftly, and without saying goodbye, stands, and turns to walk away.

After watching him walk back up the hill until he's out of sight, I curl into a ball on the grass, closing my eyes from the bright sun and the ache travelling through my heart. In such a short space of time, he's restored my sense of self-worth, and in the wake of my confusion, I already doubt whether this is the right thing.

"Mind if I sit?" The stature of my dad casts a shadow over me.

I pat the space beside me, but don't speak.

"So young Andy just told me he's off to work in Lincolnshire, said he was sorry an' all that."

"Sorry too, Dad."

"You had some sort of falling out?"

"No, not really."

He removes his flat cap and folds it in two. "You know me well enough to know I'm not big on words, Emma."

I bump my shoulder onto his.

"I just want you to know you deserve more than

anything to be happy. Whether it's Andy, or some other fella, that's all your mum and I want for you."

"I know you do, Dad. I love you."

This time I lean into him and he puts his arm around my shoulder, kissing my head. Content in his arms, I relax, until my phone vibrates.

Chris: Hey stranger. Fancy helping me again with more film festival details? C x

"Is Chris healing all right?" my dad asks.

"I think so, it's still early days, but he'll make a full recovery."

"Off you pop then."

I look up at him.

"To Chris. That's who's texting you, ain't it?"

"You don't miss much, do you, Dad?"

"I notice more than you might think," he says in return.

From behind his antique oak pedestal desk, I can see he's casually dressed in a light blue polo shirt and shorts. I've always thought the colour blue suits him. I wave, giving him a smile as I sit down on the leather sofa, where Barney joins me, and wait for his telephone conversation to finish. I've often wondered how he manages to get any work done with the views from his office windows. I'd most likely sit here and daydream all day long.

"Hey, sorry about that." Chris comes over to me, kissing my cheek, which sends a cascade of tiny butterflies through my stomach.

"No worries." I shrug it off, playing with a strand of hair. "How are you?"

"Still a bit sore. It's nice to be home, though."

"Sorry I didn't make it back to the hospital."

"I did wonder where you got to."

"I had some stuff to do and I knew Charlotte was there."

"She had to go actually, back to London for a few days."

"Sorry, I didn't realise."

"It's okay, Mum and Dad were there."

"Well, I'm just glad you're home. Where shall we start?"

"Okay." Chris turns all businesslike. "I want to show you where I propose to have the screen set up." His voice is still not fully recovered and the bruises on his face look worse. "What you looking at me like that for?"

"You just look so sore, that's all."

"I'm fine, stop worrying."

I nod. "So where are you thinking?"

"Follow me."

Outside, we come to a stop on the wide grass area near the sculpture gardens. It's the south view of the house, the one Chris's office overlooks.

"I was thinking screen over there." He draws my

attention to an area by the house. "And maybe the food and drink tent over there near the trimmed hedges. Toilets need to be at the back somewhere, over there." He points up a small hill at the far back before turning to me. "What do you think?"

"I think it's absolutely perfect. When the sun goes down you can shine some soft lighting on the house to give it a backdrop and hopefully there'll be some stars." I fan my hands in front of me and look up at the house. When I turn around, Chris is watching me.

"That does sound perfect," he says, our eyes locked together.

I quickly shake it off and look back towards the house.

"If we walk over here." Chris leads the way to the east entrance that overlooks the vast parkland. "This is where I think we should have the ticket gazebo. People can park their cars on the grass area behind it."

"Did you sort out the floodlights for the car park?"

"I did, and the attendants, plus a couple of staff who will be in the ticket tent. The merchandise and food stalls all have their own people. Have we forgotten anything?" he asks.

"No, I think it sounds very much organised." I wink. "Let's just hope it doesn't rain."

"I don't think I have any control over that, I'm afraid." He grimaces.

I give him a wide grin.

"Fancy a walk into the village? I'm having a craving for chips and this guy could do with some exercise." His voice deepens as he massages Barney's ears, whose wagging tail suggests he's already sold on the idea.

"I'm pretty hungry. Why not, but only because Barney likes the idea so much." And with that I'm almost bowled over by two excitable paws landing on my thighs.

"Down, boy—he's always preferred you over me."

"It shows he's a dog of great taste." I chuckle and chase Barney towards the house to fetch his lead.

We walk our usual route, beside the river, which Barney dips in and out of, occasionally spraying us as he shakes off the water from his coat. Along the path, there's a strong smell of freshly cut grass lingering in the air and a vibrant array of wild flowers dotted here and there. I enjoy the peaceful sound of birds singing above, darting from tree to tree. As we round a bend, I glimpse left and admire the house, just in view, stood tall and proud. The rays of the sun give it a translucent appearance that only emphasises its beauty.

From the corner of my eye, I notice the familiar arch of Chris's back and him rubbing his side. "You all right?"

"Just a twinge, it catches a bit, that's all."

"Sure you're okay to walk?"

"Yeah, can we just take it a bit slower?"

"Of course. Don't push yourself."

"I won't. Promise … So, Andy text me earlier."

"Did he?" I keep my tone level, but my body stiffens. Perhaps this, and not so much his desire for chips, was his inspiration for taking a walk—an interrogation.

"Yep. Said he's going away for a few weeks. Are you okay?" he asks, stopping for a second.

I turn towards him. His lips loitering over more words that don't seem to leave his mouth.

"We best keep moving," I say, walking on. *I don't want to have this conversation. Not with you.*

Chris falls in step beside me and we walk the rest of the way in silence.

"Let's sit and eat?" I signal to a bench in the square. Clearly, he found the walk here far harder than he anticipated and he looks tired.

"Sure."

I peel pieces of fish from the batter as I look out across the village square. There are some familiar faces milling around, nipping in the corner shop, or standing outside their cottages gossiping—a scene I'd witnessed many times over the years. The dog walkers are being closely observed by Barney; aside from this he sits, licking his lips, and patiently awaiting scraps of our food.

"When's Charlotte back?" I ask, my stomach hardening.

"In a couple of days. She wants to finalise all the wedding details, what with it being so close."

"I can't believe it's so soon."

"Well, she had her heart set on this year, after Lucy's wedding, and I didn't see a reason to wait."

More like Charlotte gets what Charlotte wants, I think, feeling that familiar burning sensation in my chest, the overriding sensation I feel when either Charlotte or the wedding are mentioned.

"Sorry, I don't want to rub your face in wedding stuff," he says, no doubt sensing my unease.

I shift chips around on my tray. "It's fine."

"I hope you really are okay, because Charlotte wants me to ask you something."

"Go on."

"I would love …" He hesitates. "We would both love it if you'll be our bridesmaid?"

My throat feels dry, like a chip has briefly lodged itself going down. "I'd love to." I swallow, forcing a small smile, but something on the inside of me shifts.

"You sure it's not too much? I'll understand if …"

"Are you kidding? I'd be insulted if I wasn't your bridesmaid," I say and tap his knee playfully, over-compensating.

He throws back his head and chuckles. "I'd have you as my best man, but …"

"It would break with tradition," I finish for him and he looks at me with bright, glossy eyes. *Please stop looking at me like that. This is hard enough.*

When we arrive back at the estate, even Barney's exhausted. Chris is pale and I know he's hurting badly, because making small talk only lasted halfway and then he fell silent.

"Do you need me to stay and do anything else?" I ask, walking through the courtyard at the side of the house.

"No, you can come in for a drink if you have time?" He's out of breath and there's a glisten of sweat on his brow.

"I best be off. Thanks, though."

"No, thank you." He leans in for a hug. The warmth of his body and the smell of his aftershave on his neckline draws me in and I don't pull back straight away.

"Emma ..." he whispers against the side of my face, but as quickly as the words leave his mouth, he stands back. I follow his gaze.

"Chris, Emma!" Charlotte is heading in our direction, looking ever-glamorous in white skinny jeans, a pale pink cross hem top and black baker boy hat.

My heart sinks to a new depth.

"Charlotte?" he says, catching her tiny waist as she kisses him full on the lips and my insides writhe, painfully.

"Emma, sweetie." She leans in to hug and kiss me Hollywood style.

I don't know what it is, but I find her slippery and insincere. Chris protests they're compatible; however, nothing I've seen, aside from them both being staggeringly beautiful, makes me see what he possibly sees in her.

"It's lovely to see you again."

I do all I can not to stiffen at her touch.

"Did you ask her yet?" She widens her eyes at Chris.

"Yes."

"And?"

"I'd love to," I interject, trying to quash their cute to and fro as quickly as I can.

Squealing, she grabs me again for a hug, then goes back to kissing Chris excitedly. The statement 'get a room' comes to mind, though the reality of this only adds to my feelings of unease.

I'm done.

"I best be off." I edge away.

"Don't leave on my account." Charlotte doesn't look up from her i-Phone, which now has her full attention.

"I was going anyway. Stuff to do."

"Thanks again, Em." Chris's stare is one that tells me he's trying to decide what I'm thinking.

Can he tell, I wonder. And what was he about to say before Charlotte turned up?

Chapter 12

The Great British Heatwave has arrived in time for the film festival, and, if it holds, for Lucy and Fynn's wedding early next month. I observe from the lawn as guests arrive, parking their cars, and forming orderly queues to pass through the white ticket gazebo. It's easy to spot those who've done this sort of thing before against those who haven't. For instance, the young couple holding hands as they enter the gazebo, carrying just a folded blanket, versus a man leaving the car park, with two chairs in bags over one shoulder, a parasol resting on the other, carrying a cool box in his spare hand. What I assume is his partner beside him, carrying only her sun hat. *Chivalry at its finest*, I think.

Both evenings have completely sold out online in advance and the daytime showings are expected to do the same if the weather remains warm. Chris appears and I pull a goofy-happy face, justified by my excitement that tonight's screening is *The Notebook*.

"Check this out." I hug him. "All your hard work's paid off."

"Our hard work," he corrects me, before kissing

my cheek and I catch the smell of his freshly showered skin, making me light-headed. "You ready?"

"Oh yeah!" I drag him down the hill, swinging our entwined hands childishly as we walk. He laughs, clutching the picnic basket that has a blanket laid neatly on top in his free hand. Carrying anything with weight even just a week ago would have been a struggle for him, but all of a sudden, he seems to be healing.

As the crowds of people thicken around us, he releases my hand and signals for me to lead the way. I'm wearing a light-blue summer dress, which clings to my newly formed curves. No longer am I skin and bone and this feels pretty good.

"There's such a buzz out here," I call back to him as we wind our way through people setting up camp with chairs and blankets, the slightly more pessimistic among them unravelling sleeping bags in preparation for a drop in temperature later in the evening. The sound of a cork pops beside us, making me jump, and I watch the man and woman laugh as they mop up the frothing champagne oozing out of the bottle neck.

I stop at the foot of a slight hill towards the back.

"Here?" I say, turning to look at the screen.

"So far back?"

"I like it here. You can take everything in and still see the film."

"Okay, but I'm surprised you don't want a front row seat to see Mr Gosling in action."

"I'll see him well enough from here."

He nods, unravelling the mat before wafting it skyward and letting it drift down onto the grass. There are two small pillows hiding in the blanket, which he leaves to one side. “There you go,” he says, holding out his hand and leading me onto the mat.

“Thank you.” I sit down and open the picnic basket.

“I recognise this spread,” I say, with a smirk on my face.

“I don’t know what you mean.” His face mirrors mine.

“I know you helped Andy with the picnic he took me on.”

He just shrugs.

“Though this is different.” I pull out a bottle of champagne. “Real fizz? Expensive, too. Shall I do the honours?” I ask.

“Here, let me.” He retrieves the bottle and pops the cork, making me flinch once more. “You’re very jumpy tonight,” he observes, pouring us both some champagne.

“I am, aren’t I? Perhaps it’s all this excitement,” I admit, smiling up at him when he passes me a glass. “You’re very well prepared, Mr Golding.” My usual statement.

“You have me well trained, Miss Millar.” His usual response.

“It’s a shame Charlotte couldn’t make tonight. She works a fair bit, doesn’t she?” I rest back on my elbows and peer up into the clouds above the house. *It’s not at all a shame Charlotte can't be here, but I can't deny that I'm curious about her.*

"I suppose being the owner of a relatively new fashion company, you have to put the hours in. Plus there's your bridesmaid's dresses and her own wedding dress that she's designed."

"I didn't know she owned the company. I thought she was a fashion designer?"

"She was before branching out alone. Her dad's financing the venture, though I think that's both a blessing and a curse."

"How so?"

"I think she'd like to be successful on her own terms. Prove to her family, mostly her dad, she can do it."

"Well, she seems pretty talented."

"She is."

There's a gleam in his eye whenever he talks about her.

"Where do her parents live?"

"The family split their time between the UK and America, have done for years. That's where she was for a few months when you first arrived home. We'd got engaged before she went to America."

"Oh, I see." I swallow hard. "Why the States?"

"Her dad's a big business tycoon out there, with lots of connections and plenty of money, of course."

"So how did you meet?"

"Charlotte's parents are old family friends and were invited to a dinner at the estate. We sat together and got talking, then a few weeks later we sat together again at another function. Over the course of about six months, we built up a relationship, I guess. We do have a lot in common, you know."

"Like both of you are ridiculously rich and attractive."

"Well, I'll take the attractive compliment, thank you. Listen, I know you're worried. I'm a big boy, though. Big enough to know what I'm doing."

"It's not that."

"What is it then?"

Now would be as good a time as any.

"I, urm … will that be it when Charlotte comes back for Lucy's wedding—I mean, will she be staying from then until your big day?" *Sigh.*

"Yes."

I sip my drink. "Have you decided on a honeymoon destination?"

"Jamaica. One of her friends owns a resort out there."

I raise an approving eyebrow, but reverting to small talk seems to have frustrated him.

"Emma …"

"It's starting." I clap my hands lightly together as the screen comes to life. As I turn away from him, I'm not sure whether to feel saved by the timing or deprived. Either doesn't sit well in the pit of my stomach.

When the sun fades, the sky turns from grey to black,

creating beautiful silhouettes around the trees. The house is softly lit as I imagined it would be and the only other light is coming from the big screen and the food tent on the periphery.

"Here." He shuffles over, unaffected by our previous conversation. He lifts his arm for me to rest on his chest as a cool breeze descends upon us. Thankful for the dark to hide in, I snuggle into his side, aware this may be the last time we can do this.

We're fast approaching my favourite kiss in the rain scene.

"It wasn't over." Chris mimics the film ahead of the lines, as if reading my mind.

I lift my head up to glare at him. "I'll hurt you," I say, resting on my elbows. My hair falls across my face so he pushes it to one side, stroking the side of my face with the palm of his hand. I involuntarily lean into his touch, the nerve endings throughout my body starting to tingle.

"It still isn't over," Chris whispers in time with the film as I hover inches from his mouth, his breathing as quick as my own.

"Shush!" Someone calls out as we jump apart to the sound of Chris's phone ringing loudly. He stands in haste to answer it away from the crowds.

"Everything okay?" I whisper when he reaches the blanket, kneeling beside me.

"Not really. That was the home." His gaze is unfocussed, his voice soft.

"What home?"

"Colin's home, Em. He's passed away."

The next day, I'm sitting beside Chris in Colin's room. He'd taken care of all the formalities this morning. We had no idea Colin had named him next of kin, though this shouldn't have been a surprise; there was no one else. All that's left to sort out now is his belongings. We'd brought boxes, although we wouldn't need many. He'd lived a simple life and always had. Rose was the one who liked to collect 'little knickknacks' as she liked to call them. After she died, Colin wanted to get rid of everything. He'd told us we could keep anything we liked, but the rest should go to the charity shop. I chose four delicate white porcelain dolls, with long painted eyelashes, holding a colourful flower, that were no bigger than a couple of centimetres in height. Rose kept them in the kitchen on a shelf and I used to play with them as a young girl. I'd always loved them.

"It's so strange." I shake my head.

"I know."

"They're both gone. I was only here with him a couple of weeks ago and I was planning on coming over today to tell him how the film festival's going," I say.

"I can't believe it either." He's staring at an empty box by his feet. "He seemed fine when I saw him just this week, tired perhaps, but fine."

"I know," I say, picking up a pack of cards which had caught my eye. "Do you remember these?" My breathing slows.

"Happy families." Chris gives a slight smile. "Stephen used to love that game."

"Master Bun, Miss Cod, Mr Stamp, Mrs Corn, Master School." I flick through the deck. "Rose and Colin were like an extra set of grandparents to us, weren't they?" I say, remembering how attentive they both were.

"They were."

"I wish I got to say goodbye." A tear rolls down my cheek and I catch it with the palm of my hand.

"Hey, he knew how much he meant to us. We meant a lot to him too." He strokes my arm.

I close my eyes and dab more tears with my fingertips. "We best get organised then," I resolve.

Chris is taking down the frames from the dresser, most of which are photos of Colin and Rose, bar one. A photograph of Stephen, Lucy, Chris and me. He picks it up and I notice him rub his thumb over his brother's face before placing it inside the box.

"I'm sorry."

"What for?"

"For being a terrible friend after Stephen died. I wasn't there for you and I'm sorry."

"You don't have to apologise."

"I want to. We were never as close afterwards, until these past few months. I hadn't realised how much I'd missed it."

"Me too …" I feel words rising up from somewhere deep inside me, but now isn't the time. "We should probably crack on."

"Yeah."

There's a flat atmosphere in the car on the drive back. I just stare out of the window in silence. Only the sound of Chris's voice breaks me from my trance.

"Want me to take you straight home?"

I shake my head; being alone right now is the last thing I want.

"We could catch what's left of the film at the festival?"

I can tell from his tone he doesn't much feel like it, but then I figure he doesn't want to be alone either. We are both taking Colin's death harder than we're letting on.

"I know where we can go." He changes his mind about the film without needing my input.

After a pit stop at the house, we leave the car and walk into the grounds of the estate. I don't ask where we're headed, but just follow his lead. The noise from the film drifts into a gentle hum on what's another warm and bright summer's evening, though all I feel is cold.

"Here."

I've paid so little attention, I only now notice where we are as I look up at the old treehouse Colin built, what feels like a lifetime ago.

I stare up at it, my eyes prickling with tears.

"We used to spend hours in there. Do you remember?"

I feel him look at me, but I'm still staring.

"I think we once spent the whole summer in there playing board games and hiding from our parents," he adds.

"Yeah, but there was a time when it was boys only and you and Stephen wouldn't let me in."

Laughter fills the air around us now at the bittersweet memory.

"Let's go inside?"

"You first."

"I remember it being bigger."

I join him and notice he's rubbing the top of his head. The centre of the treehouse is high enough for standing up, but the edges aren't, least not as adults. "Sit down before you bang your head again."

He does as he's told.

"What's that?"

He pulls a bottle from the box. "The 1950 Bordeaux wine he told us about. It was in his wardrobe."

"We don't have a corkscrew."

"Ah ha." Chris reaches back into the box. "What I stopped by the house for, along with a couple of blankets."

"Are we staying here all night?" I tilt my head to one side, pursing my lips.

"Who knows? Like old times, I thought." His smile builds slowly.

I look through the rest of the contents of the box while he opens the wine and take out the photo frame of the four of us together, setting it in the corner alongside the photo of Colin and Rose.

Chris hands me a filled glass.

"To those who are no longer with us."

"To Colin, Rose, and Stephen," I say and we raise our glasses together.

He leans against the side of the treehouse. "Here." He pats the floor in front of him, inviting me to lean back on his chest. I shuffle happily into position and rest back, my head in the crook of his neck.

"It seems such a long time since we were up here last, so much has happened," I say, hearing Chris take a deep, savouring breath.

"This place has so many memories, good and bad."

"It really does." I pause, a touch of sadness in my tone. "You said before 'like old times'. Do you remember when we spent the night out here? We told our parents we were staying at each other's houses, but instead we decided to sneak and camp out?"

"We did, didn't we?" His face lights up like a lantern as I twist to look at him.

"Lucy wouldn't join us because she 'didn't do camping' and Stephen didn't because he wanted to stay in and phone his girlfriend."

"Rebecca Johnson," I add.

"Yeah, I hated her," Chris scoffs.

"Do you remember eating so much we felt sick?"

"Dandelion and burdock, bacon-flavoured Wheat

Crunchies, and 1p pick-and-mix sweets from the village corner shop."

"I don't think I drank dandelion and burdock ever again after that night. The burping!"

He pokes me in the ribs.

I jolt. "That was you," I insist.

"If you say so," is what I hear, but I feel the jitters of stifled giggles from his ribcage.

"If I remember correctly you were a bit of a wimp."

"How dare you!" I pretend to be affronted. "It was so cold and dark that night."

"You always were scared of the dark. The amount of times you jumped and said, 'What's that?' I'm surprised you lasted as long as you did."

"We both got fed up and cold, walked back to the estate and snuck back to your room before your parents had even gone to bed."

I don't need to see his face to know he can see that night with the same clarity as me, as if we have our own private screening of it on the treehouse wall.

"Shush, don't tell anyone that."

He whispers so close to my ear that I get a shiver that doesn't cease until it reaches my lower spine.

Later that evening, when the wine has all but gone, I can hear the recurrent chirp of crickets and the tree branches brushing against the roof in the breeze. When an owl lets out an elongated screech, making me flinch, Chris switches on the lantern.

"Scaredy cat."

I elbow him once more and he holds me tighter. I think about all the times we've lain here together and it fills me with a mixture of sadness and comfort remembering how much these four treehouse walls have seen us through.

"We always come back to each other, you and I." He speaks softly, invading my own thoughts. As he runs his fingertips up and down the length of my arm from my shoulder to my elbow, my heart beats quickly against my ribcage.

"You and me forever …" I twist my body to look back at him from my place on the floor between his legs. His brows are pulling in. "Don't frown," I say, stroking his forehead. My breathing quickens alongside his as he traces the outline of my face and I close my eyes.

"It's getting late … I should probably be getting home." I breathe out, shuffling onto my knees.

"That's probably a good idea," he says as he stands, holding out his hand to help me up.

My vision feels as if it's lagging behind my movements, which reminds me how drunk I feel, alongside a pang of guilt creeping up from my toes, intensifying by the second.

"I think we're both just a little over the limit, so I'll call you a taxi."

"It's okay. Dad will still be up. I'll give him a bell now."

"Emma …"

"Chris, let's just put it down to the wine, or the treehouse and a little too much nostalgia, okay?"

"Okay."

Chapter 13

My phone vibrates on the bedside table and I wake to its sound. *Lucy*. I place it face down. She called me yesterday requesting I be at the estate for nine o'clock sharp. My bridesmaid's dresses, *plural*, are ready and she and Charlotte are going to be there this morning for my fitting. Needless to say, I feel as much like having my dress fitting with Charlotte as I do gouging my eyes out with a spoon. If anything, I'm leaning towards the latter, it would be far less painful.

A week has passed since my evening with Chris and I can still feel my heart thumping against my chest whenever I think about his warm arms wrapped around me, stroking my face so tenderly. My breath catches in my throat as I close my eyes and see his face, inches from my own just moments before I pulled away. All too quickly, though, my thoughts are replaced by those of Chris with his fiancée. How seeing them with each other makes my insides churn, with both guilt and jealousy that do not sit well together.

Rolling out of bed, I make my way downstairs, with sluggish, heavy steps. Opening a kitchen cupboard, I stare at the cereal boxes for a few seconds before closing the door. I open the fridge and take out the carton of orange juice, pour myself a tall glass and elbow the door shut. As I sit on the sofa cupping the glass in my hand a text from Lucy pings. I don't need to read it to know what it says. I know I'm in trouble and I need to get a move on, but I don't want to see Charlotte. She's marrying the man I'm in love with. The man I want to be with so badly he makes every fibre in my body ache, so that I have to use every ounce of willpower to walk away from him.

By the time I pull into the car park at the estate, it's nearly ten. I'm thinking how late I am, when my phone rings again. Swinging into the car parking space, I reach down into the passenger footwell to retrieve it from my bag.

"I'm here, call off the dogs." I hang up before Lucy can make any comment.

Once inside, Lucy lifts her arm and taps the expensive rose gold designer watch on her wrist.

"You're late."

"I'm sorry, I'm here now." I pause, noticing Elizabeth in the room.

"Morning, darling." She moves towards me, kissing my cheek.

"Good morning."

"Morning, Emma." Charlotte's hands are full of papers and fabric swatches.

"Morning, Charlotte," I reply without making eye

contact. I'm grateful she doesn't join in the welcoming hugs and kisses. "Where do you want me?" I ask, dropping my bag on the floor by a chair.

"Your dresses are laid out in the bedroom. Hopefully they'll fit you without needing too many alterations, and you like them, of course," she adds, albeit with a conceited tone. As if to imply I couldn't dislike something she'd designed.

In the bedroom, I find two dresses hanging on a rail. I trace my hand over the fabric of my bridesmaid dress for Charlotte's wedding and my heart sinks. *Charlotte and Chris's wedding.* I make a conscious effort to draw my attention away to the dress Lucy has chosen for me to wear for her wedding. It's the one and only time I've given Lucy free rein in this department and it's not what I expected. The one shoulder, knee-length gown is not quite orange in colour and has an almost Arabian flamboyance to it. The back is low cut and at the front, from the waistline up, it's crowned with crystals that reflect the colour through them. I have to admit it's magnificent.

As I re-enter the room all I hear is the proud gasp that leaves Elizabeth's lips and all three women stand to attention.

"What's this colour, Charlotte? It's absolutely stunning." I can't help but sound sincere.

"Persimmon, as in the fruit."

"I love it."

Charlotte gives a haughty shrug.

Lucy rushes over to me and lifts my hand to twirl

me around. "You're going to be my bridesmaid." A tear trickles from her eye.

"Aren't you supposed to cry when you see yourself in your dress, not me in mine?" I reach for the tissue box and offer it to Lucy before taking one for myself.

"Mine isn't ready yet, so that will have to wait, but I'm so happy I could burst." She grips my hand tighter.

"I would like to see my future daughter-in-law in her wedding dress, if I may?" Our attention is drawn to Elizabeth and Charlotte huddled together, smiling.

"Oh, but we need to see Emma's other dress …"

"There's time for both," Elizabeth interrupts.

"Okay. I'm dying to show it off to you all. We need to move quickly, though. The boys will be here soon."

"The boys?" My shoulders tighten.

"Yes, you were late," Charlotte declares in a shrill tone.

"We told them to come by at ten-thirty to collect us, thinking that would be enough time." Lucy finishes the telling-off that Charlotte started.

"What for?"

"Emma!" Lucy scolds me further, but I don't know what I'm supposed to have forgotten. "We're all going into the city for the suit fitting and then out to lunch, remember?" I can't quite decide if she's scowling or frowning; either way, I keep quiet.

I watch Charlotte disappear into the bedroom to change and if I hadn't still been wearing my bridesmaid dress, I would have made an excuse to leave. Seeing her in her wedding dress is not what I need right now, none of this is.

Lucy disappears into the bedroom to assist, and as the door re-opens, a beautiful bride emerges, followed by a fishtail train. I'd expected modern, but this dress, with its abundance of lace and embroidery, has a vintage look. The batwing sleeves give it a sort of Gatsby glamour and all I can visualise is Chris's face when he sees her.

Lucy touches Elizabeth's arm, who is awash with tears.

"Mum, are you okay?"

She dabs at her eyes with a handkerchief. "I'm just so happy, that's all." Lucy hugs her and Elizabeth holds out her hands for Charlotte to join them.

"Emma." I hear my name. "Do *you* like it?"

"Charlotte, you look amazing."

"Do you think Chris will like it …?"

My eyes are stinging, but I swallow hard. "I think … he's gonna love it." I force a sincere tone, but to my surprise, the words leave me more easily than I thought they would. *What wouldn't Chris love about this, a stunning bride and a happy mother? How can I ruin it?*

I retreat into the bedroom to change, craving time alone, which is short-lived as Charlotte pushes open the door to join me.

"The boys are here, so I need to get out of this dress before Chris sees it. Will you help me undo the buttons, please?"

"Sure."

Charlotte is beautiful, with perfect hair, perfect

skin, and as I observe her slipping out of her wedding dress, the perfect figure. My chest burns.

"Try on your other dress," she insists, changing into her normal clothes.

Barely keeping it together as it is, I do as she wishes, though I want to hide. The sound of Fynn and Chris in the next room isn't helping.

"Are you ready, Emma?" Lucy asks, through the door.

I hesitate in front of the mirror in the simple antique pink, cowl neckline, cap sleeve dress that seals my fate. Then I step into the room full of the audience I don't desire and look at no one.

"Beautiful!" Fynn declares.

I feel the blood rush away from my extremities, the result of which is a heavy tingling sensation in my finger tips and I wring my hands to try and dispel it.

"Do you like it? Will you feel comfortable in it?" Charlotte appears in front of me, holding my wrists. My skin temperature soars. *She's so smooth, especially in front of Chris and his family.*

"Of course I like it, both dresses are magnificent. You're very talented."

She lifts her shoulders and beams at me before turning to Chris.

"Do you like it?" she asks him.

Chris hesitates for a fraction of a second, his lips parting as I flick my eyes up to look at him involuntarily.

"It's beautiful," he says quietly and the sound of his

voice makes my heart start to splinter.

Charlotte makes a sound, almost like a hamster squeaking, and then quickly engrosses herself in excited conversation with Lucy and Elizabeth.

Our eyes immediately leave one another, and as I turn away, I notice Fynn staring in my direction. I hastily leave the room. With the door closed behind me, I rest my burning skin against the cool wooden frame, almost gasping for air.

The car journey into the city only exacerbates the awkwardness I felt back at the estate. Lucy and Charlotte are seated to my right. Fynn is in the front passenger seat and Chris has a perfect line of sight towards me in his rear-view mirror. I don't need to look up to feel the weight of his glances at me. My eyes, however, are firmly fixed on the moving horizon of buildings as we draw into the city. I still don't understand why I have to be here, politely suggesting as much back at the house, but it's clear from Lucy's response that I had to come along. Despite myself, I know it's just Lucy's way of making sure I feel included, but then she doesn't have the full story.

"I'm starving," Fynn announces, climbing out of the car once we reach the car park. "I vote we eat first?"

"No arguments from me," Chris adds. "Ladies?"

"We have time. I know a great restaurant," Lucy

says, grabbing both my and Charlotte's arms as if we're all the best of friends. In passing, Chris's eyes meet mine and yet again Fynn is watching.

Pierre's restaurant is a modern French bistro with harbour oak flooring and distressed wood panelling on the walls. The table where we're seated has a cerulean blue leather bench on one side, with matching fabric chairs on the other. The wall in front of me holds a chalk board with specials announced in elegant handwriting. Either side hang two large mirrors with grey frames. The reflection in one of the mirrors is a wrought-iron staircase at the far side of the room and a white lantern-style light, hanging from the ceiling.

I'm at the bar not long before getting served. I'm sure the waiter would have brought me a drink to our table, but I needed an excuse to be away from our group. As I rejoin them, Lucy pulls swatches from her bag to show Fynn the fabric for the boys' suits. I watch with some amusement as she tries to coax him into her choice of colour. 'The choice', because despite any remonstration from Fynn there will be no movement on Lucy's part, is a three-piece electric blue suit, with a cravat made by Charlotte to match my exotic fruit-coloured bridesmaid dress.

"I would laugh, but I assume we're all having *that* forced upon us, Sis?" Chris asks, slapping Fynn on the back. I can't help but laugh out loud with him. He looks over at me and for a brief moment, we're just two friends laughing at something funny the other has said.

"And if by *that* you mean my exceptionally impeccable taste in suits, then yes, Christopher."

"I love it," Charlotte pipes up.

Of course she does.

"Thank you." Lucy shoots Chris a smug grin.

"Tell us more about your honeymoon, Charlotte. We still can't decide where to go, can we, Fynn?"

Fynn just shakes his head. I gather from this he's not fussed and it's Lucy who can't quite decide.

Charlotte takes out her phone, "I'll show you some pictures. It's divine. Aquamarine seas, white sandy beaches."

"Wow, just wow! Fynn, you have to see this resort." Lucy pushes the phone in front of him and he makes all the right noises.

"We can climb straight out of bed and down into the water from our very own overwater bungalow, can't we, darling?"

Can't we, darling. Gag.

"Apparently so." Chris smiles at her.

I'm all burnt-out with wedding and honeymoon talk, yet this is still on the menu, it seems. "Can I get anyone a drink from the bar?" I need to excuse myself somehow.

"Didn't you just get a wine?" Chris looks down at my empty glass.

"Wedding plans make me thirsty, I guess," I say, ignoring his harsh squint that tells me to slow down.

Everyone else's okay for drinks, except Fynn, who joins me.

"How you holding up?" he asks.

"I'm fine." I know Fynn is both suspicious and astute, so I'm not sure how I'm going to fob him off.

"I can't imagine this is exactly what you want to be spending your time doing at the moment? I certainly didn't want a bar of weddings for some time after my divorce."

"No, you're right, it's not easy." I feel as though Fynn is building up to something and I'm right.

"This might be none of my business, Em, but I'm sensing something's off with you and Chris?"

"We had a falling out before his accident." I wave, trying to get the attention of the barman, who is busy at the opposite end of the bar.

"I thought that's all behind you guys?"

"It is." I shift, leaning over the bar to make my presence further known. Thankfully, a man with a face full of designer stubble starts in our direction.

"Madame, what can I get for you?" the barman asks in his rich French accent.

"Rosé, please." I look behind me at our table and see Charlotte's hand resting on Chris's thigh. "Make it a large, please," I add. "Fynn?"

"Nothing for me, thanks."

The barman measures the wine into the glass and presents me with it. "Shall I charge it to your table?" he asks, scribbling on a notepad.

"Please," I say, not needing to clarify which table. As I turn away, Fynn lightly touches my arm.

"If you need to talk to someone, I'm a pretty good listener."

I pause. "Thanks, Fynn, but I'm fine."

"Just be careful, Em. Neither Lucy nor I want to see you hurt again."

"I know." I breathe in and walk off.

Fynn's right. I'm already hurting.

Chapter 14

Looking through my window, I spy Fynn's Range Rover before hearing the honk of the horn. It's early Saturday morning and the day of Lucy's hen party, which means a full day relaxing at a spa, followed by a meal for all her family and friends later this evening. Lucy opted not to have the meal at the estate, as is tradition. Things have been tense since she announced setting the date, so I don't blame her. Instead, the meal is to be at her friend's Italian restaurant in the city. I, for one, am relieved not to have to endure being at the estate; neutral territory is fine by me. Even better than that, I'm spending the day alone with Lucy at the spa. No Charlotte, or anyone else for that matter.

The sun's out and already there's a warmth to it as I lock my front door. The weather has certainly held since the film festival and now the wedding is only two weeks away. It's almost too nice to be locked in a spa all day, but Lucy assures me there's a perfect place outside with some sun loungers for a spot of sunbathing.

"Morning," I greet them both, avoiding any sort of

eye contact with Fynn, who I haven't seen since the day of the dress fitting.

"Morning," Lucy chirps back as I lean into the front to hug her.

"Excited?" I ask.

"I'm so excited I could literally burst." She claps her hands together several times, making her look like a hungry seal. "In just two weeks I will be Mrs James Fynn," she says, squealing in a higher pitch than either Fynn or I'm prepared for and making us jolt in our seats.

"Morning, Emma," he eventually says. "I think you're going to have quite a day with this one."

"Hey!" She pokes his shoulder playfully, and he takes her hand, kissing her palm.

Fynn drops us outside the entrance to the spa, which is just outside the city. We've transport sorted for tonight in the form of a hot pink stretch limousine, entirely to Lucy's taste. Our small suitcases on wheels are packed with our best 'out out' clothes and a tonne of make-up to the point where it looks a little as if we're staying here for a few nights and not just using the facilities all day.

"Good morning, ladies. How are we today?" the tall, slim, blond ponytail-haired man behind the desk asks us with a wide smile.

"Very well, thank you," I reply. "Our spa day's booked under Millar. Here are our health questionnaires." I slide them over the counter.

"You're both my favourite people this morning for completing these forms in advance." He turns his back for a second, long enough for Lucy to nudge me.

"He fancies you." She tips her head in his direction.

I nudge her back just in time before he rejoins us, clutching two hessian bags.

"Here are your goodie bags, ladies. In them, you'll find your robes, slippers and a towel. If you need to exchange them throughout the day I'd be happy to oblige."

"I bet he will!" I hear Lucy mutter.

"Beth will show you to the welcome lounge where you'll be served a glass of champagne to get your day started," he continues, without noticing Lucy's impromptu mutterings. "Then one of the team will be down to run through your itinerary for the day." He pauses, looking at me long enough that I blush.

"Thank you," I say without meeting his eyes.

"Thank you," Lucy says more playfully, making up for my reticence.

Linking hold of my arm, we follow the petite ash-blonde-haired lady in a black outfit.

"Here we are." We're directed to a vacant round table near a window, overlooking a terrace. Our champagne flutes are set in front of us by a boy in a white polo shirt, who doesn't linger long enough to be thanked.

It's not long before one of the beauticians appears, wearing the same black cropped trousers and straight collar tunic as Beth, who'd seated us.

"Morning, *ladies*, my name's Ariel. How's the champagne?" She immediately strikes me as a little over-zealous, especially for this early hour.

"Perfect." Lucy sits tall, beaming at her, and I feel guilty for my lack of cheer.

"It's perfect, thank you," I agree, trying to rally my spirits.

"So, who's the lucky bride-to-be?"

Lucy squeezes her shoulders together and points to herself.

"Lucy, welcome, and congratulations." She hands us both a sheet with our itineraries on. "Okay, so, *ladies*, you have your champagne welcome already, check." She makes a mid-air tick gesture to emphasise the 'check' and I'm cringing on the inside. "At midday, you'll have your three-course lunch in *La Brassiere*, which is through the double doors on the left," she says, indicating much like an air stewardess during the safety demonstrations on a plane. "At one p.m., it's your Swedish body massages and personalised facials, all with our delicious range of luxury products. At four p.m., you will have manicures, pedicures, and hair styling ready for your big night out." And with that, she brings her hands together in a clap. "Any questions, *ladies*?"

I have just a couple: like how many times was she going to say 'ladies' during our conversation? Also, would she sing? Perhaps a rendition of: 'Part of your world' from The Little Mermaid*? I stifle a laugh, knowing it would upset Lucy that*

I'm being this mean-spirited for her hen party day.

Despite how I feel on the inside, I do think the itinerary looks impressive and both Lucy and I love a good facial. Spa days were usually Lucy's treat for my birthday, though it's been such a long time since our last spa day together.

We spend the morning rotating the various rooms, of which there are many. I always find the steam room most relaxing, the sauna a bit too hot for my taste, and, as always, the scented rooms are my favourite—particularly the room smelling of lemongrass. Most of the rooms are softly lit, with sounds from nature, or pan pipe music playing quietly in the background, enabling me to drift off into another existence entirely. We don't pay much attention to the 'keep quiet' signs when alone in the rooms, but do respect it when joined by other guests.

After leaving the stream room, I step into an alcove and press the silver button on the wall beside me. What tension remains soon evaporates, feeling the cool mist surrounding my skin, followed by jets of warm water cascading over my body. It is accompanied by claps of thunder and the soothing sound of torrential rain increasing in intensity, before filtering back out again as the shower comes to a stop.

"We should do this more often, like we used to," Lucy says when I join her in the dim candle-lit cave pool.

"I agree," I say without hesitation, as the warm waters engulf my refreshed skin.

"So how do you feel about seeing Andy in a couple of weeks at the wedding?"

The sound of his name causes a disagreeable knot to form in the pit of my stomach. In truth, I hadn't given much thought to Andy's return. My mind has been otherwise engaged.

"I think I'll be too busy to notice." I give her a wry smile to try and avoid this line of questioning.

"Do you miss him?"

And … it hasn't worked.

"I don't not miss him, if that makes any sense, but I'm not sure that's the same as missing him?"

"Maybe you can talk to him at the wedding?"

I'm finding it increasingly hard to lie to her. "I dunno, Luce, it's more complicated than that." And with that, I push off the underwater seat and swim to the steps, Lucy fast on my heels.

"Is there something you're not telling me?" she asks, falling in step with me as I walk towards the door and out into the sunshine to find our sun loungers. "You just haven't been yourself lately and I've had this odd feeling you're hiding something?"

The truth's on the tip of my tongue. "My divorce came through yesterday," is what I allow myself to say instead, not that this isn't the truth. It is. The post was sitting on my mat when I got in from work.

"Why didn't you call me?" she asks, perched on the edge of a sun lounger.

"I didn't want to spoil today for you." Which is only a half truth. The one person I'd wanted to call was Chris. My thumb had hovered over his name on the screen until I'd thought better of the idea.

It wasn't what I'd expected, then again, I hadn't really known what to expect from my divorce being finalised. Perhaps a fanfare announcement that years of marriage had officially come to an end. When you get married the photographer wants to photograph you both signing the register. All of your family, your bridesmaids, and the best man are in the picture celebrating it with you. When you get divorced, you get an envelope with a piece of A4 paper inside. One single piece of A4 paper and it just doesn't seem enough. There's one line I've read over and over: '*that the said marriage was thereby dissolved*.' Dissolved … evaporated, finished, melted away like snow, there one day and gone the next. I'd allowed myself to cry, though it was for a shorter time than I'd expected. After that, I filed the piece of paper with my other important documents, and with some irony, alongside my marriage certificate.

"You should have called me, I would have come over."

"I'm fine. I didn't even cry as much as I thought I would, really."

"That's not the point." Her eyebrows knitted together. With the sun scorching hot and not a cloud in sight, it makes for a rather clammy cuddle as she leans over to me, almost upending her sun lounger. I grasp her shoulder more tightly and she breaks into fits of giggles.

"Is there anything I can do?" she asks me, more

composed.

"Not really, but thank you for asking."

She squeezes my hand. "Does Chris know?"

"No," I say a little too indignantly and she jerks her head back, opening her mouth to speak, but a voice interrupts.

"*Ladies*, ten minutes until lunch is served." It's Ariel from earlier.

"Thank you," we chorus, as Lucy turns to me, pushing her sunglasses to the end of her nose.

"I wonder how many times a day she says, *'Ladies'?*"

This time, I'm the one who breaks into fits of giggles.

"What did I do?"

"Nothing, Luce. You just made my day is all."

Lunch was delicious and we're both somewhat tipsy when we arrive for our massages shortly after our third glass of champagne that day. A beautician leads us into a dimly-lit room, the sound of string instruments playing softly in the background. In front of us waits a second beautician, who looks remarkably like the first, standing bedside two beds. Lucy must be thinking the same as she looks back and forth between them.

"If you can remove everything down to your pants, lie face down on the bed, and cover yourself with the towel, please?" they say, almost in sync and I can hear Lucy's breathing rate change as though she's desperately trying not to laugh.

"Are they twins?" she asks, slipping out of her robe and onto the bed.

"They have to be. Surely?"

We both stop talking the second we hear a knock and the pair re-enter.

"Is the pressure too firm?" my masseuse asks after I flinch a couple of times early into the massage.

"No, not at all, I'm just a little ticklish." I try to focus on my breathing until my skin acclimatises to her touch. Once relaxed, I drift in and out of awareness, enjoying the sensation of soft hands gliding up and down my oily skin. With each stroke, the pressure in my temple builds and then dissipates, leaving my body.

Now I'm feeling the most relaxed I've felt in a long time and have decided never to leave here. Despite currently waiting to have my fingernails filed and polished, it's hard to imagine getting all dressed up to go out tonight, especially given that I could happily crawl into bed this second. More wine should do the trick, though probably not until later, or I'll definitely be too comatose to participate in the festivities.

Lucy and I are back to small talk and my relief that she hasn't tried to start anymore conversations about Andy, or Chris, is short-lived, because her next topic is worse.

"You don't like Charlotte, do you?"

The question comes from nowhere and blindsides me completely. "She comes across as nice enough."

"Is that the sum total of your assessment about the

woman who's marrying one of your best friends?"

"What more do you want me to say? She's stunningly beautiful, seemingly intelligent, rich, and well-bred." My delivery hadn't been supposed to sound so peppered with jealousy.

"Em, are you sure there isn't something you're not telling me? I mean, I feel as if you're struggling with more than just your divorce coming through. You didn't really want to talk about Andy, or Chris, and he's been in an odd mood lately. Are you jealous?"

"Jealous?" I flinch.

"Of Charlotte? I know Chris was jealous when you and Matt first got together. He may have been busy, off with lads all the time, but he still felt the change in dynamic of your relationship and I know you once had more feelings for him than just friendship."

"Yes, once upon a time I did have more feelings for him. I didn't know he'd struggled that much, though."

"He stomped around the house for weeks around the time you went public with your relationship. I told him to get a grip and that it was bound to happen sooner or later, though he just told me to mind my own business. You know what he and I were like back then. Stephen had always been our buffer, so to speak. We didn't do so well with one another for a few years once he'd passed."

"Well, I have felt a little out of place since I learnt about their engagement. Chris hasn't really done the serious girlfriend thing when I've been around and we don't seem to know how to be friends when either of us is seeing other people."

"I guess that was always going to be the problem with a boy/girl friendship. Least you never had sex."

I swallow my own saliva so fast it chokes me.

"Em, you all right?" She places her arm around my shoulders and I'm relieved to be wearing a thick robe so that she can't feel the heat coming from my skin.

"Yeah, I don't know what happened."

"I'll fetch you some water."

Lucy had known about my feelings for Chris years ago. I never went into too much detail, because she's his sister and their relationship was never an easy one back then, so I don't think she ever understood how serious I was about him. Every part of me wants to tell her now. Tell her everything, but I can't. Ruining her happy mood on her hen party is not an option. Mostly, I can't tell her, because I'm not even ready to admit to myself how close it came to something happening between us.

The limousine arrives at the front of the spa shortly after seven. The table's booked at an Italian Restaurant for half-past, where twenty-five of Lucy's close friends and family are gathering for her hen party. The car is large enough that we could move the party inside it, especially given how well stocked the mini-bar is. Most people are meeting us at the restaurant, but Lucy and I are making a few stops en route, meaning by the time we arrive, we're fashionably late. Lucy neither notices, nor minds, settling into her favourite role of being centre of attention. I have to admit, it's nice to have 'the eyes' off me for the time being, and more importantly, it's ladies only tonight.

"To the future Mrs Fynn," one of Lucy's friends offers as a toast, which is followed by chinking of glass and excitable squeals. So far this evening, I've chatted with several of Lucy's close friends and people I've known from years gone by. Almost all are married and have children, or are expecting one. Suffice to say, the evening is like an awkward school reunion I wish I hadn't attended and the only thing masking the depressed feeling rising from my core is the copious amounts of prosecco I've drunk. Every conversation either starts with, 'Are you married?' for those I've completely lost touch with. Or, 'How's Matt? Oh, I am sorry,' for those who I've been in touch with since school, but not since my separation. 'Do you have children? Oh, don't worry, people are having them much later in life these days,' usually signals the end of the awkward conversation. It's ironic how much I want children now, given how little I did back then. Strange to think that if things had been different I would have a five year old now and it makes me wonder what life would look like? Child or no child, I'd still be divorced and that would make me a single mum. I think, though, perhaps I would prefer that, because at least then I would be a mum, instead of living in this lonely void.

"More bubbly, Emma darling? I turn to see Lucy's aunt standing behind me holding a bottle. I noticed her across the room earlier, but she'd been engaged in conversation with Charlotte and Elizabeth, who I'm doing a sterling job of avoiding. After Stephen died, Aunt Sarah stayed at the house for a good few months, so we had the opportunity to spend a great deal of time together.

"Aunt Sarah." I try to stand, but I'm being trapped by the table, the tightness of my dress, and far too much alcohol to coordinate the movement.

She kisses my cheek.

"I'd love some. Thank you."

"How are you?"

She may well be the first person to ask me that question without the sympathetic head tilt that normally accompanies it.

"I'm getting there." I give her a warm, thankful smile.

"Are you sure? If I didn't know better I'd say you look woeful in a way that can only mean one thing—a man." When it comes to love, Aunt Sarah is intuitive and exceptionally blunt.

"I'm just tired. Lucy and I were at the spa early this morning and I'm ready for my bed."

"Nonsense, I could party all day and night at your age. You'll perk up with some more of this." She passes me my refilled glass.

"Have you met the groom?" I ask.

"Fynn? Yes, such a lovely chap. Handsome, too, which is always a bonus. I approve of Lucy's choice immensely, despite my family's reservations."

"Ah yes. A divorced person, not high up on the Golding check list of eligibility."

She shrugs.

I know Aunt Sarah is a realist. She married for love, not money, which took her to Australia to be with her husband, Hugh. They have no children, though I've never asked if this is through choice or circumstance. I imagine the latter.

"Lucy's choice is a darn sight better than Chris's," she says.

"Do you not approve?"

"My darling girl, I don't approve of a lot of things around here, but it's not my place to interfere. I'm merely here to enjoy the weddings of my niece and nephew and to spend some time with the people I care about."

I'm still thinking about what Aunt Sarah said later that evening as Lucy appears, carrying two shots.

"You seem a bit out of it?"

"I'm just flagging. I think all the relaxing at the spa has made me sleepy," I say.

"This ought to help." She hands me a shot glass.

"What is it?"

"Limoncello. It's my hen night and you're not nearly drunk enough."

I sniff the shot, downing it without hesitation.

Several limoncellos later, the numbers have thinned and the remaining hens pile out of the limo and into The Groovy Club's VIP lounge, where we've spent many nights dancing away to the club's retro music. Lucy has been customarily dressed up in a pink and white veil, garter, and L plates before being dragged onto the dance floor by a very drunk friend, whose name escapes me. Two other hens are busy rating men at the bar with a hen party card game, whereby you score someone 1-10 (1 being 'Complete Minger', 3 is an impressive 'I'm Drunk Not Blind', 6, 'Tasty' and 10, 'Hit The Jackpot'.) Things must have been going well, because one of the girls holds up a 10 for us all to see and starts kissing a stranger's face off. I'm not so sure, I would give him a 3 at best, but she's in a far worse state of inebriation than me, just. I consider going over to stop her from making a mistake, as I spot someone familiar at the bar. *Chris.*

I'm not sure what possesses me as I march over, almost stumbling into him in the process. He turns, placing both hands on my shoulders, and I realise I must be swaying.

"Emma." His eyes lock with mine. Those deep, searching eyes. I want to tell him to leave the eyes out of it, but in my present state I'm not sure it makes any sense, other than in my head.

"Christopher!"

"I'll leave you to it, mate." A short, dark-haired man pats Chris on the back and makes his escape.

"Emma," Chris repeats, an ever-growing smile on

his face.

Was this funny to him? "Don't mock me, Christopher."

He laughs. "Here, sit." He gently guides me to a bar stool, making sure I'm steady before letting go of my arms.

"What are you doing here?" I rock backwards, but correct myself.

"Pint of water, please." Chris signals to the barman. "I was having a drink with a friend, but you seem to have scared him off."

"Oh, sorry." I draw back. "But you don't even like retro music."

Chris ignores my comment, sliding the glass of water in front of me.

"Here, drink this."

"I'm not drunk, Christopher!"

"Only drunk people say that. Drink up," he insists.

I reluctantly do as I'm told and down the whole pint in one, making an 'ah' sound.

"Very clever."

"Stop mocking me."

"Wow, you really are making an angry drunk right now. What has my sister been feeding you?"

"Well, first bruschetta, then salmon al p … p … p …"

"Peppe?

"That's the one. And then lemon jelly shots."

Chris tries, but fails to stifle his laughter.

"You mean, limonchello?"

"That's what I said, didn't I?"

"Okay." The smile is firmly fixed on his face.

"You won't be smirking if Lucy catches you crashing her hen party, or your wife."

"Fiancée," Chris corrects. "And I didn't know you would all be here. I'm just leaving anyway, since you scared off my friend."

"Sorry about that."

"It's okay. It's far more entertaining watching you drunk." His eyes are lit with a warm inner glow. "Seriously, though …"

My heart rate picks up pace as I think of all the things I feel unable to say to him. How can I tell him that his eyes catch me off guard every time, almost breaking my resolve? Or that right now, his lips are screaming, 'kiss me', and the scent of his aftershave makes me feel more intoxicated than any of the alcohol I've drunk tonight.

"Christopher Golding," Lucy bellows, with both hands on her hips. "This is my hen party. No men!" Lucy makes a shooing gesture.

"I didn't even know you were going to be here, Luce. Don't worry, I won't cramp your style."

Charlotte notices Chris and runs towards him.

"Chris!" she screeches, flinging herself at him with such force he seems winded as their bodies meet.

"Wow." He peels her off. "Hi there, you're a little bit worse for wear, aren't you?"

"I think you should take her home," Lucy says.

"I don't want to go home!" she protests, but her

head slumps onto Chris's shoulder.

As Lucy hugs Charlotte goodnight I look at Chris, wishing there was no one else here aside from him. Wishing it was me he had to take home, instead of her.

"Night, girls. Love y'all!" Charlotte announces, one arm raised, waving her shoes above her head.

"Come on." He takes the shoes, wrapping his arm around her waist.

As he walks away, I notice him look back at me.

Chapter 15

The estate church is beautiful even at its plainest, like today, for Colin's funeral. There's only standing room left inside, a testament to how well loved he was. I'm staring at the crimson rose wreath resting on the box where his body lies and missing him terribly already. I can't look at Chris, he hates funerals even more than I do. Death seems unfair, though not in Colin's case. After all, he'd 'lived a full and meaningful life', or that's what he always said if any of us got sentimental about the idea of losing him one day. In many ways, I knew he was just biding his time until he could be reunited with Rose. I dab my eyes to stop tears from falling, needing to keep it together for my reading. So far the service has been very fitting, taken by the local vicar, who often visited Colin at the home and knew Rose also. A tear has been glistening in his eye since the opening hymn, threatening to fall any moment.

"Now we will have a poem." He signals to me and I rise to my feet. Colin had asked me to read Rose's favourite poem at her funeral, but I was too upset. This time, with red eyes and trembling hands, I step forward, gripping the bookmark that Rose had once given me, though I know this off by heart.

"God hath not promised skies always blue,
Flower-strewn pathways all our lives through;
God hath not promised sun without rain,
Joy without sorrow, peace without pain.
But God hath promised strength for the day,
Rest for the labour, light for the way,
Grace for the trials, help from above,
Unfailing sympathy, undying love."

"Better late than never," I whisper, almost to myself, and I can hear Colin saying 'Timing is everything', as he always did. Dabbing a tear from my chin with the back of my hand, I notice, on my way past, the vicar doing the same.

Following another of Colin's favourite hymns, which I'm too choked to sing, it's Chris's turn to step up to the pulpit. He places a sheet of A4 paper on the lectern and clears his throat.

"Thank you all for being here today. I know Colin would have been touched you all came to say your goodbyes to him, though he always said he didn't want any fuss when he died. 'Just bury me with my Rosie,' he'd say, 'none of this big send-off business'." Chris smiles and looks at the coffin in front of him. "I'm sorry, Col, we couldn't let you go without a little fuss." There's a ripple of quiet laughter.

"I had the privilege of knowing what a true gentleman this man was." He stumbles over the word 'was' and has to take a breath before continuing. "A wise man, a hard worker, a husband who was second to none and a great friend. I didn't always see him this way. I used to see this grumpy old man who told my brother and me off and stopped us from playing.

We gave him quite a hard time back in the day, hiding behind plant pots as we squirted him with water pistols, or purposely kicking our football into his flower beds. We hid his tools and sometimes his lunch box." Chris closes his eyes as if to recall the memory more clearly. "Once, Stephen opened his lunch box and found some homemade cookies. We shouldn't have, but we ate them all, and were so scared he'd find out that we put his lunch box in the bin to hide the evidence. We never did own up to it—until now."

Once again, quiet laughter fills the pews.

"The summer that Stephen beheaded a row of prizewinning roses, Colin decided to build us a treehouse and we realised how special he was. He introduced us to Rose, the maker of the tasty homemade cookies, and we saw a different side to him. A fatherly side. It was sad to hear they couldn't have children of their own. I always thought what a fantastic dad he would have been. Rose would have been a wonderful mother too."

My chest tightens as I swallow down heavy sobs.

"Colin and Rose were family. They celebrated with us when we were successful and cried with us in our misfortunes. The world is a darker place now that you're no longer both in it, but heaven, as you believed it to be, has gained another wonderful soul." Chris turns one final time to where Colin is resting. "Thank you …" He inhales. "For always being there for me and for the joy you brought to all our lives." He shakes his head, his voice wavering. "I know you're happier now, back with your Rosie … We'll miss you," he says, gathering up his paper. As he passes the coffin, he touches it and takes his seat by his mother.

The mourners drift away from the grave leaving only Lucy, Fynn, Charlotte, Chris, and I. Holding two roses, one white, one red, I look down into the grave where Rose is already buried, now beneath Colin. The crisscrossed rose stems resting on top of the coffin remind me of a conversation I once had with him about the meaning of all the different colour roses. He told me that when a white and a red rose are given together it signifies unity. I throw them in side by side, as a symbol that Colin and Rose are now united once more, forever.

"We should get back to the house. Everyone will be up there soon for the wake," Lucy suggests in a small voice as Fynn kisses her on the forehead.

"You guys go, I just need a few minutes." I'm staring at the dug-over pile of dirt.

"Will you be okay?" She touches my arm.

"Yes." I give her a half-hearted smile and she nods, letting Fynn lead her away.

Everyone leaves, aside from Chris, who steps beside me without saying a word.

The sun's at its highest in the sky and the air feels heavy as I breathe in. The last time we'd stood here was at Rose's funeral, which had been a harsh winter's day. I hadn't wanted to leave her because I said she'd be cold and alone.

"You okay?" he asks.

"I feel as if I keep losing the people I love." I turn to him. "Sorry, you don't need me to tell you about losing people."

"It's fine, you're allowed to grieve, Em."

"I feel as if all I've done this year is grieve." I begin crying. "And cry." I shake my head.

"Hey." He pulls me towards him in that all-too familiar way of his, but I don't stay long in his arms.

"I'm okay." I step back, reassuring him.

"You read well," he offers as conversation as we start to make our way back to the house.

"Thank you, I felt as if my voice was cracking."

"It didn't show."

"Your eulogy was beautiful."

"I hope I did him justice."

"You did."

He stops me with his hands. "Talk to me?"

"My divorce came through," I tell him, walking away to sit on a bench under a tree.

"When?" he asks, joining me.

"The other day."

"Why didn't you say anything?"

"I don't think I have anything else left to say about it. It made me sad to see it in black and white. I cried for about twenty minutes, which was not as long as I thought I would cry for. Now I feel relieved. It's over, the line drawn. It's robbed me of enough time and happiness."

"I'm in awe of you, you know." He turns his body, our knees touching. "I've watched you these past few months, everything you've become. You've grown. No one would have blamed you if you'd rolled over and given up, but you didn't. You carried on. I think you're an incredibly strong, amazing woman, Emma Millar." He strokes my face and for a second I look into his eyes and see a flash of warmth that almost instantly retreats into something resembling regret.

I stand. "I'm going to go home."

"What about the wake?"

"Will you tell people I was too upset and wanted to be alone?"

He leans forward to get up, but I give a small shake of my head and he realises I've made up my mind.

What he doesn't realise is how easily he could change it.

Chapter 16

The bridal party move into formation at the top of the aisle as Canon in D, by Pachelbel, strikes up. As the last of Lucy's entourage, I'm directly in front of the bride and Sir Richard. One foot at a time, I step along the thick burgundy carpet in time with the music and of all the eyes in the room, there is but one pair I meet. A breathless sensation washes over me instantly and I want to look away, but I can't. In that moment, no one else exists. I reach the foot of the aisle and round to the left, taking one last fleeting glance at Chris before my attention is on the bride, with everyone else.

Lucy is a vision in a white princess dress, her face obscured by a long veil and her father's expression says it all. He's the proudest man that ever lived. I see tears in Fynn's eyes and I have to dab my own away with the back of my hand, pressing the length of my fingers under my bottom eyelashes to preserve my mascara. Sir Richard lifts her veil and holds his daughter's bare shoulders before kissing her on the cheek. He turns, shaking Fynn's hand and the ceremony begins.

I'm offered a glass of champagne as I enter the marquee. In front of me, a radiant Lucy is holding the arm of her besotted husband, Fynn, greeting guests. During the ceremony, I was able to forget my situation on a couple of occasions. Outside the church, however, I opted out of the bouquet-throwing tradition with the other single ladies. When Charlotte caught it and celebrated with Lucy and Elizabeth, I snuck away, and ever since, I've been busying myself.

No sooner than I've taken a sip of my drink, do I see Andy heading in my direction.

"Hey stranger." He leans forward, giving me a lingering kiss on the cheek.

I blush. Despite everything, he still has some effect on me.

Since his departure a couple of months ago, so much has changed and I'm not sure what he's expecting from me, or what I'm going to say to him if he asks about us, which he will.

"How are you?" I ask.

"Really well, thank you."

"You're looking tanned, I assume from outdoor life and not a holiday?"

"Correct. It's been pretty good weather, hasn't it?"

"Absolutely."

"Are you well? I mean, you look well." He rubs his neck and I think his skin reddens a little under his tan.

"I'm good."

I watch as he tries to work out what other pleasantries we can exchange, but deep down I know he's building up to it and I'm not ready. I'd thought about how I might feel seeing him again and it surprises me that I still have feelings for him, given everything. If only I didn't feel as I do for Chris, Andy and I would stand a chance, but he deserves better than to be someone's consolation prize.

"I'm kinda out of small talk." His fingertips lightly brush a strand of hair from my cheek. "What I really want to tell you is how beautiful you look."

"Andy …" I stare at the floor.

"I'm sorry. I was trying really hard not to pressure you, but seeing you." He touches my arm and my skin tingles.

I pull away and his head lowers. "It's so good to see you, it is. I just can't talk right now, okay?"

"Sure." He edges away, holding my eye contact for as long as possible until he disappears into the crowd of guests.

"Hey." Lucy tugs at my arm and pulls me into a hug. "There you are."

"Sorry, I was just talking with Andy."

She grimaces. "Do we need a debrief?"

"Maybe?"

"I have something to tell you too."

My eyes widen. There could be only one thing, aside from getting married that would make her this excited. "Are you pregnant?" I whisper.

She lifts her finger to her lips, nodding wildly. The grin spreading across her face is so wide it's in danger of splintering her cheekbones.

"I'm so happy for you." I throw my arms around her and whisper in her ear. "Does Fynn know?"

"Yes, but it's really early days still. He's finding it hard not being able to announce it to the world, but we want to wait until after the first scan. We'll tell close family, but we didn't want to tell them even, until after the wedding. You know the fuss Granny would cause. *A divorced man and a baby out of wedlock*," she imitates quietly, making me chuckle.

"Honestly, Luce, I couldn't be happier for you."

She kisses my cheek, "Fynn and I wanted you to be the first to know. He would have come over with me, but like I said, he's about ready to burst and I'm not sure he trusts himself enough to tell anyone, just in case."

"I won't tell a soul."

"Anyway, I just wanted to make sure I found you in case I don't have time later, before we go away on honeymoon."

"So does this mean I get to be Aunty Emma?"

"Absolutely." She wiggles her shoulders. "I need to get back to Fynn. You were right about the day going quickly, I already feel as if it's slipping away."

"Enjoy every second, Luce. Make sure you take a moment to look around and remember it all."

"I love you, Miss Millar."

"I love you too, Mrs Fynn."

She squeals and swishes off.

I retreat into the toilet where I lock the door and lean

against it. I'd meant every word about being happy for Lucy and Fynn, of course. Now though I feel guilty, guilty for feeling jealous of my best friend's good news. There's nothing more I want right now than to be happily married, with my own family, and despite how much healing I've done in the past few months, this hasn't changed. I haven't stopped wishing I was someone's wife, or mother. Weddings and news of babies just make my losses more poignant and remind me of the choices I've made up to this point in my life. Choices that have cost me my happiness.

There's nowhere to hide during the speeches, but at least they're not boring, funny even. Sir Richard, followed by Fynn, then Lucy, who had to have her say, of course. She had wanted me to say a few words, but I'd declined—no great surprise. I'm not known for my love of public speaking; it had been a rare thing for me to speak at Colin's funeral.

Chris's speech is being received well and I can't help but laugh out loud during his run of jokes at Fynn and Lucy's expense. However, aside from that, I try to keep my expression unreadable.

"I just want to say a few words about someone who can't be with us today, but who I know would very much loved to have been. All of you who knew our big brother, knew he loved an occasion such as this. In fact, he was made for them. I'm pretty sure he would have given a far better best man's speech and made you all laugh more than I." There's a rumble of quiet enjoyment and Lucy tilts her head warmly as Chris takes her hand in his. "Stephen would have been so proud of you today, Luce." He shakes his head, his emotions threatening to take hold as they had at Colin's funeral. "And I know just how much he would have approved of your choice of husband," he says, giving Fynn a nod. "So I'd like to raise a couple of toasts if I may … to Stephen, we miss you, buddy." Chris raises his glass to the sky and his eyes follow.

"*To Stephen*," the guests chorus.

I'm now a puddle of snot and tears, along with all the family members seated at the top table.

"My second toast is to the happy couple. Please will you all be upstanding and join me in raising your glasses, to the bride and groom." Chris raises his own glass.

"*The bride and groom*," another chorus of voices shout, as the air fills with cheers, clapping and whistling.

This perfect summer evening is what Lucy wanted when she planned to hold the reception in a huge marquee in the estate grounds. As it turns out, this is exactly how she envisioned it would be. Crisp white linen tablecloths and chair covers with orange bows tied around them. White roses and orange picasso lilies, to match Lucy's bouquet, sit in tall vases at the centre of each table, surrounded by petals, crystals, and church candles in differing sizes. Above the large wooden dance floor the ceiling twinkles with fairy lights as though it's the night sky filled with a thousand stars. The band, which play covers of songs, has been playing for an hour with some brave guests taking to the dance floor early, though most were still absorbed in their conversations and the flowing alcohol. I search the room, not for the first time this evening, hoping to catch sight of Chris.

As I weave my way through the tables, I see him emerge at the edge of the stage and speak to a member of the band, before turning in my direction.

"Hey," he says, reaching my side. "I need to find Lucy. They're announcing the first dance and Fynn can't see her anywhere."

"She's probably just in the loo," I reassure him, moving my fingers around my charm bracelet.

"I wanted to check you're okay? You've been really busy all day."

"You know your sister, she's a slave driver." I don't smile. "It was a lovely speech," I add, though my tone sounds far colder than usual.

"Thank you."

I hear the first dance music begin and turn to see Lucy being led onto the dance floor by Fynn.

"Ladies and gentlemen, it's time for Mr and Mrs Fynn to take to the dance floor for their first dance. They have specifically asked that the best man and maid of honour, Chris and Emma, join them in the second half of the song."

My body stiffens as people encase the dance floor and us. The room lights up with the flash of cameras as Fynn twirls Lucy and dips her low to the floor. He's miming the words and she's beaming up at him adoringly. I still can't seem to move and I fear there's no escaping what's next.

"Shall we?" Chris holds out his hand to me after seeing Lucy give us the nod, sooner than expected. *Why all of a sudden did she want to share the limelight?*

I hesitate for a moment before taking it.

Our bodies meet in perfect silence on the dance floor, as he places one hand on my waist, keeping hold of my right hand. It's been a month since he held me and every part of my body aches to stay here in his arms. I inhale and close my eyes for a second as he circles his thumb gently around the exposed skin of my lower back. I imagine his gentle lips on mine, though they do not meet, and when his thumb rests, I look at him, falling into my favourite of his features—his eyes. The crowds all but fade away and so, too, the consequence of anyone seeing something between us.

All too soon, the music changes tempo and people flood the space around us. I step back quickly, as if waking from a trance and before we can speak Charlotte appears.

"Can I steal him from you, Emma?"

"Of course." I smile and turn my back on Chris.

At the edge of the dance floor I stop to see him

dancing with her. She's kissing his neck and making more of a display of affection than normal. Perhaps she'd already drunk too much and we're in for a repeat of the hen party.

I need some air.

Stepping onto the bridge, I can finally breathe for what feels like the first time today as I inhale the night air. It's been hectic, not to mention a bit of an emotional rollercoaster and my stomach agrees. Though I can't decide if I feel sick through stress, too much alcohol—or both. This wedding's been difficult enough and I'm not sure how I'm going to survive Chris and Charlotte's. Right now, at least, as I rest both hands on the comforting coolness of the stone wall, I'm pleased for the opportunity to be alone.

The night is slowly sinking in around me as I listen to the sound of nature being fused with faint music. The bright summer moon reflects on the river below and the lamps at either end of the bridge attract night flies which make small sounds as they bounce off them. I hear the incongruous sound of the gate creak and turn to see Charlotte walking towards me.

"I saw you head in this direction," she says, reaching me.

"Oh," is all I reply, feeling as if my solitude has been invaded.

"I'm just going to get straight to the point, Emma. I

saw you two dancing together."

My throat is dry and I can no longer move my feet.

"You see, Emma, Chris loves me, regardless of whatever's going on between the two of you. Him caressing your back and you staring at him like a hopelessly infatuated schoolgirl. I'm really not bothered who he shags before the wedding."

"Charlotte …"

"Just listen!" Her tone is dark. "You see, I quite like the idea of a title." She looks up, drawing a line in the air with her thumb and first finger. "Lady Charlotte Golding. It has a certain ring to it, don't you think? Owning a thriving country estate such as Wincastle and his family name will be good for business. And at least now I don't have to pretend to be faithful."

I feel as if I'm stationary and the bridge is swirling around me. "What are you talking about?"

"Oh, Andy didn't tell you? He and I are a little more acquainted than you might think."

"You're lying."

"Sweetie, did you think I was marrying Chris for love? Men can't resist me and they usually do what I want them to." She slides both hands down either side of her figure.

The gate creaks open again and I see Andy running through it.

"Hey, are you okay?" he says, wrapping his arm around my shoulder, but I shrug him off.

"Maybe you should ask Charlotte, given how well you *know* each other!"

"What are you talking about?"

Rolling my head back, I close my eyes tight. *Will this horrible day ever end?*

"You told her?" he asks Charlotte, rocking back.

My blood feels as if it's draining all the way to my toes.

"I think given that she's having sex with my fiancé, she's not too bothered."

"Firstly, Chris and I have never had sex! So, you can forget about using that as your pathetic excuse for sleeping around. Secondly, Charlotte, maybe you should crawl back into Daddy's pocket, and while you're at it, take Andy with you!"

"Emma." He moves in front of me, blocking my path. "Sleeping with Charlotte was a mistake, it's you I wanted to be with. Admittedly at first it was a bit of a game to mess with Chris's head, because he'd always told me to stay away from you, but …"

"Excuse me, what?"

"Emma …"

"A bit of a game, are you kidding me?"

"I said at first," he splutters. "Not when we got to know one another, pretty much from our second date."

I can't handle any more truths tonight.

Not wanting to hear any of this, I turn away and see Chris emerge from the shadows, walking towards us.

"Perfect timing, Arsehole," Andy says. Then unsuspectingly he's thrown backwards under the weight of Chris's blow, clean on his chin. Crouched low, Andy spits blood on the ground as Chris flexes his right fist. Neither looks away from each other. He spits again, rubbing his chin, head cocked to one side as he rises to his feet. In Chris's eyes, I've never seen such fury as in this moment. This fight is Chris's to lose and I can see from the look on Andy's face that he knows it.

"Stop!" I scream, my shout echoing across the bridge.

"Is it true?" Chris turns to Charlotte. "Did you sleep with him?"

"I never promised you I'd be totally faithful."

"It's in the vows we're supposed to take on our wedding day in two weeks!"

"Exactly. We're not married yet, Chris. Can't we just call it cold feet and forget all about it and I'll pretend I haven't seen how you look at her?" She glances towards me.

Chris breathes out slowly.

"I'm sorry, Charlotte, it's over!"

"You think you're breaking up with *me*?"

"You slept with someone else, and yes, I'm in the wrong, too, because I've been having feelings for Emma, but I didn't act on them, because I loved you. I asked you to marry me because I thought we were good together and I hadn't felt this way in a long time. Perhaps I don't know you well enough after all."

"I'm too good for you anyway," Charlotte says as she turns her back and trots off the bridge, Andy not far behind her.

Chris starts walking in the opposite direction and I follow him, taking off my shoes to keep up as he picks up speed. I know where he's going and I don't stop until I reach the top of the treehouse ladder and see him standing there.

"Emma."

"I'm not leaving you alone, if that's what you're going to say."

He shakes his head. "… You can say I told you so, if you like."

"Why would I? You never did after Matt left me. Besides, we both fell for charmers this time around."

"I'm sorry Charlotte cheated on you with Andy. Are you okay?"

"I think I punched him for hurting you actually."

"Chris …"

"Em, listen. I meant what I said on the bridge about having feelings for you …"

"Chris, I was in love with you all those years ago, before you went off the rails after Stephen died and cast me aside like an old shoe."

"What?"

"I get you were grieving after Stephen, I do. I was too. And I know you apologised for it when we were packing away Colin's things. We'd grown so close in the months before Stephen's death and afterwards you just disappeared. It was as if the person you used to be was no longer there. You didn't show me any emotion, or anyone else for that matter, except the dozens of women I had to watch you parade around with on social media. Only I had to grieve losing you too. When Matt came along, he swept me off my feet, he listened to me talk about losing Stephen—things I hadn't been able to say to you. Things I should've been able to say to you. I wanted so many times for you to reach out to me. It was only after telling you I was pregnant that you mustered up any kind of a reaction. I was so angry with you, Chris, because then it was too late. Part of me thinks I married him anyway just to hurt you, like you'd hurt me. Well, that backfired, didn't it!"

"Emma, I never meant to make you feel as if I'd cast you aside, I had no idea that's how you felt. Back then was a truly awful time in my life and there's something I never told you. My mum tried to kill herself after Stephen died."

I inhale louder than intended.

"She wrote a note and took a lot of tablets that she'd been prescribed for her mood, mixed with some alcohol. I was going to tell you when we were at Colin's, but I couldn't find the words and you were already so upset."

"What happened?"

"I found her."

My hands fly up to my mouth and cover it.

"They rushed her to the hospital. She was in a bad way."

"Chris, I had no idea."

"The whole thing really messed me up, hence the partying and shutting myself off from everyone, especially you. The women you mention were just girls we joked around with at parties, mostly who my mates hooked up with. I was too broken to get involved with anyone. I had no idea you thought this of me. I'm sorry.

"You don't have to explain …"

"I do. Emma, I was so in love with you before all that happened. I remember kissing you the night before we found out about Stephen. I know I was horrendously drunk, but not enough to forget that. I'm so sorry I abandoned you." He steps forward, his body inches from mine in the centre of the treehouse. "We always come back to one another, you and I." He speaks softly, his hand tracing the outline of my face. When he reaches my lips with his thumb, he draws a line down them and they part, before placing his mouth where his thumb has been. Lingering against their warmth, I can taste the fruit and spice of wine on him as he gently moves his lips over mine. The silent beats of my heart are no longer as silent as he pulls me towards the floor and onto his lap, kissing me intently now. With every stroke of his lips, I lean into his body. He unzips my dress, before smoothing his hands down over my shoulders, taking with them the strap, making every inch of my skin feel a warm prickle. With every kiss of my neck, I moan quietly in his ear, a noise his body responds to. My fingers are tingling as I fumble at his shirt buttons before peeling it from his shoulders, brushing my lips across his chest. I stop suddenly and he opens his eyes to find me looking at him.

"Chris."

He slides his fingertips once more along the line of my mouth, silencing me.

"Stop talking," he utters, grazing my lips with his as we lie down.

Chapter 17

I wake to the sound of my alarm and lie here, watching him sleeping, undisturbed. The room is light from the early morning sunshine trying to force its way through the blinds in my bedroom. We've not left the house much in the past seven days. In fact, we've not left this room much since our night together in the treehouse, after Lucy's wedding. Chris and I made love for the first time in there and it was just as I imagined it would be. Perfect. I can't count the times since, we have a lot of years to make up for, and I don't want this time together to end. I don't want reality to seep in and taint what we have right now, in this moment.

He stirs in a familiar way and his eyes find mine.

"Morning," I say.

"How long have you been watching me sleep?"

"Not long."

"Isn't it stereotypically the man who watches the girl sleeping peacefully?" His eyes twinkle with mischief as he shuffles towards me.

"Perhaps …"

As his mouth finds mine, I lean into his body, returning his kiss as if our lips haven't met in days, not just a few hours.

"I think we're starting to have a problem." I push back strands of fallen hair from my face and sit up.

"This is my kind of problem, if that's what we're calling it." His smile gets sexier by the second and I know I need to get out of the bed and into a very, very cold shower if I'm to try and make it into work this morning.

"Some of us have jobs to go to. I don't exactly work for myself."

He tries to grab my waist and pull me back into the bed, but I escape.

"Technically, I work for my father and the board of trustees, if we're being accurate. Can't you call in sick?"

"Calling in sick my first day back after a week's holiday—yeah, that won't look suss at all."

"Okay, but I want to see you later. I could cook you dinner at mine?"

"After a busy shift, all I'll want is a quick dinner and a bath."

"Sorted. Come by after work and your wish shall be granted."

I lean over and kiss him.

"I just don't want to spend any more time without you."

"Me too. I'll see you later."

My feet are on fire as I pad my way to Chris's apartment later that evening, though my stomach has the good kind of butterflies fluttering around in it. The kind that makes you feel as if you're superhuman and can survive without food, or sleep for days on end. Normally while the sex completely takes over every spare hour, and some hours that aren't so much spare, as reassigned temporarily. In fact, I spent a good part of my day at work trying to fight off the flashbacks and cheek-aching smiles that accompany them.

"Hey," I say, seeing him emerge from the bathroom. Within seconds, he's in front of me, pulling me in for a kiss. Forcing my mind back to the many places it's visited today.

"Your bath awaits you, Miss Millar."

I follow him and see in front of me a full to the brim bubble bath, with tea light candles dotted around the room and a champagne flute resting on the side. Some Boyce Avenue acoustic covers play quietly in the background.

"Thank you." I turn and put my arms around his neck, kissing him.

"You get sorted and then your dinner will be ready."

"I thought I said just something quick."

"It's a Chinese. Delivered any minute, so totally on brief."

I laugh and feel that all too familiar ache in my cheeks.

"Why are you smiling at me like that?"

"Because all of a sudden, I'm not so hungry."

He walks towards me, scooping his arm around my back, pulling me towards him as his fingertips find the buttons of my top.

"What about the Chinese?"

"It'll keep …"

"Yum," Lucy says, as I pass her a glass of diet coke. Both of us are perched, crossed-legged, on her king-size bed in the new marital home she and Fynn share.

"I guess this will be the only fizz we share in the next few months." I know how much not being able to drink will bother her.

"Dismal, isn't it, but worth it," she says and the look on her face as she massages her stomach makes something stir inside me. It's already plain to see how much Lucy's in love with this baby.

Fynn and Lucy arrived back from honeymoon late last night and it wasn't long before she messaged to ask for a catch-up tonight, alongside kicking the boys out to the pub to do the same.

"So, debriefing time?" she says, using a napkin to wipe her lips after taking a bite of her pizza I picked up on the way, following her plea to 'Bring pizza!'.

"You want all the sordid details of my and your brother's fledgling romance?"

"Well, you can spare me those, but I want the non-physically intimate highlights, yes."

"I'm not sure there's been many of those in the past month!" I laugh and flop back onto the pillows of Lucy's bed, where she joins me, the pizza box on the sheets between us.

"I'm ridiculously happy. The kind of happy that makes you want to talk about it constantly to anyone who'll listen."

She squeals in a very Lucy fashion and almost squashes the pizza box as she leans over to hug me.

"So, perhaps we might be sisters for real!"

"Luce, come on. We only just got together. Let's not run away with those kinda ideas."

"Okay, okay. I'm allowed to hope though, right?"

"Well, I suppose we can all do a little of that."

She squeals again and I shudder.

"Seriously though, I want to take things slow this time. Finally just enjoy being with him, and the butterflies … and the sex."

"Woah—too much information. I think you burned my ears!"

I laugh so hard my sides start to ache and Lucy's the same.

"You and Fynn seem so happy. I loved all the exceptionally cute honeymoon selfies you posted online," I say when the laughter subsides.

"We are. It's like this baby has brought us even closer together."

"I can't wait to meet him, or her. I'm going to spoil them rotten, I hope you realise this?"

"I wouldn't have it any other way!"

"Do you think you'll find out if it's a boy, or girl?"

"I think we'll leave it as a surprise, but we have a while to decide. My first scan is in just under a month."

"That's exciting. How've you been feeling?"

"I was fine most of the honeymoon, just more tired than normal. I felt queasy on the flight home and again this morning, so I'm hoping it's not the start of morning sickness."

"Well, it'll pass if it is and I can help you if you don't feel well."

"Thank you. What would I do without you!"

After clearing the pizza box and drinks away, I climb back onto the bed beside Luce, who is falling asleep. The boys are still out, so I decide to snuggle down myself and wait for Chris and Fynn's return.

An hour later and the moonlight is seeping into the room, creating shadows on the walls. I check my phone and notice a message from Chris, telling me they're on their way home and he'd pick me up when he drops Fynn off. Slipping out of bed, I tiptoe into the en suite bathroom and check myself in the mirror, noticing that I've smudged mascara under my eyes from crying with laughter. I riffle through some cupboards to find Lucy's make-up wipes to rectify the situation when my hand stops on a home pregnancy test box. I lift the box from the cupboard and stare at it, thinking back to breakfast, and how, for the past couple of mornings my tea tasted off, so much so that I didn't even bother to make one this morning. Tonight I'd wanted to eat all of the pizza and then some, and even now, I'm still hungry. I feel as though an army has marched up and down on my eyelids, my boobs are sore, and … I'm late.

I lock the bathroom door, clutching the test in my hand.

Loitering in the quiet bathroom, I hope there's enough time before Chris phones to tell me he's outside. The plastic stick is face down on the edge of the basin and I daren't touch it, as if it's hot, and to touch would lead to me getting burnt. I drum my index finger against my lips and stare it down, willing it to turn over by itself. If only Lucy weren't asleep and I could ask her to look, though that would mean telling someone, instead of musing over this idea alone. I reach out my hand and pull it back again, take one large, deep breath and spin the stick over.

Pregnant … not again …

"Did you girls have a good evening?" he asks, the dark car my only comfort right now.

"Pizza, girly film and a chinwag, of course. You?"

"Spent most of the evening talking about you, actually."

"Poor Fynn!"

He laughs and I breathe more easily.

"He's so happy we finally got together and he doesn't have to hide his suspicions about us from Lucy anymore."

"Hope he wasn't in the doghouse over it?"

"No, she said he should have told her what he thought, but it's not like he knew anything for definite."

"Their baby's going to have no chance keeping anything from its dad!"

"Poor kid! A teacher and spy for a dad!"

"Lucy talked a lot about the baby. She's so excited."

"Fynn, too. He's the doting dad already."

"Uncle Chris, hey. Bet you're excited yourself? I know I am."

"Absolutely, I can't wait to meet the little one. Take it for walks, feed it chocolate, and teach it all the things I know will annoy Luce."

"Ha-ha."

"You think I'm kidding."

"No, I don't doubt you're true to your word!" I smile at him through the moonlight resting on our faces. "No doubt she'll be roping us in for babysitting duties."

"I'm fine with babysitting. At least I get to hand them back at the end of it. I said to Fynn he's way cooler about becoming a dad than I'd be."

I place my hand on my chest to try and calm my heart rate, feeling waves of adrenaline surging through me the more he says. I've never asked Chris if he wants children. He knows I do, but perhaps this is something we should have discussed before starting this. I want to speak, but every word feels stuck in my dry throat.

"Em, did you fall asleep on me?"

"No, I'm pretty tired, though."

"We'll be home soon."

Nothing more is said by either of us, as the layers of confusion, stacking so high inside me, start to make me feel trapped. My hands, shielded by the darkness, find my stomach.

I want you.

Chapter 18

Seven months later ...

There's a strange atmosphere in the car on the way to the hospital for the scan, heightened by the silence between us. Things haven't been the same since he found out about the baby. After the shock wore off, he'd said all the right things about wanting a family of his own and becoming a father, though I'm not sure we're doing the right thing. It's all so complicated, what with the wedding and everyone being so disappointed in us, my own uncertainties are rising in me like a flooding reservoir.

The silence continues, sitting in the waiting room, surrounded by anxious, happy faces and women with varying-sized bumps. Elated couples walk around the corner clutching their first photo of their babies and it saddens me I don't instinctively feel that way.

"Emma Millar," the sonographer calls my name.

Entering the dimly lit room, I'm greeted with a pleasant smile from her.

"Okay, Emma, if you could lie on the couch, lift your top and lower your trousers a little, please?"

I shuffle onto the couch, doing as she asks.

"This may be a little cold," she warns as the gel lands on

my stomach, making me flinch.

I'd been sick first thing and again after my toast. Now all I'm left with is an overwhelming nausea as I try to concentrate on my breathing to see if it will pass. My full bladder is only adding to my discomfort, alongside being weak and tired from the lack of food. Thankfully, I've managed to keep the water down, however, I suspect the fact that it's sloshing around in my empty stomach is not helping my nausea.

"Are you sure of the dates you gave the midwife, Emma?"

"Yes, I'm very regular, always have been." I look to the screen again and see a bubble shape, but it's empty. "Is there something the matter?"

The sonographer keeps silent as she rotates the probe harder and deeper into my skin.

"What's that?" he asks, referring to the bubble shape.

I already know what's happening—the bubble is empty.

"I'm sorry to tell you both this, but there's no baby."

My eyes fly open, there's a bead of sweat on my top lip and my T-shirt's wet.

"Em." Jo pushes open the door and turns on the light.

"It's okay. I'm fine," I reassure her.

"That dream again?" she asks, perching on the bed beside me.

"Yeah." I sigh and reach for the glass of water on my bedside cabinet. As I take a sip, Jo reaches out and touches my belly. "This little one's fine, it's just a dream."

"I know, but they feel so real. Matt was there this time and it was just as it happened all those years ago."

"You have the midwife today, don't you?"

I nod.

"Well, I've done some googling and having vivid dreams in pregnancy is normal, but maybe ask your midwife about it just to put your mind at ease? I need to go to work. Try and get some more sleep." She kisses me on the head.

"Okay, Mum," I say, teasing her for mothering me of late, though I've been grateful for it in the past few months.

Jo's already dressed for work and when I check the time, it's six a.m. If it wasn't for needing the loo, I would stop in bed and try to sleep as she had suggested, but the dream disturbed me too much for that.

Aside from hideous morning sickness and now some pretty horrid night-time indigestion, my pregnancy's been fairly uneventful. Last time the midwife checked me, my blood pressure was raised. I'd been having the dreams then also, but forgot to mention it to her. The fact that my blood pressure's creeping up isn't reassuring, so the nearer my due date, the more anxious I'm becoming. Staying relaxed had been the prescription from the midwife, though it's harder than it sounds. One of the only things that seems to relax me is to go for a walk on the beach. It's early, but as I can't sleep anyway, I decide to get dressed and go before my appointment.

The beach is empty and my boots sink into golden sand as I make my way to the wall I like to perch on. From there I watch the brave, or somewhat crazy surfers bob up and down on their boards in what I can only imagine is the coldest of seas, and my skin feels as though it's tightening at the thought of it. The peace and privacy of the beach at this time of year is what I enjoy, before the tourists descend in the summer months. The south-west coast of Cornwall, or the jewel of the south as it's sometimcs referred to, is so beautiful. On a hot summer's day, when the sun shines on the clear bluey-green ocean, you can easily forget you're in England. My mind remembers fondly the many holidays taken here with my parents as a kid. Chris, Lucy, and Stephen had joined us, too, on the odd occasion.

Today the sky is clear, the air crisp and the sea is a dark blue, with a hint of grey. I wrap my scarf tighter around my face as I watch two surfers sink below a wave on their way back out to sea. It's forecast snow for most of the country, but here there is none. Still, it's too cold to be out there in the ocean, as much as I envy their freedom. I miss how my body worked when I wasn't pregnant. The simplest of tasks are now so difficult, such as bending over to put on or remove a pair of shoes, or bending over in general. Walking has turned into a waddle and I've given up on shaving my legs. No one sees them anyway and no one will, until the birth. Leading up to then I might enlist Jo's help in that department. I'm looking forward to the day when

I can sleep on my back, or sleep period, though I know it will be unlikely with a newborn baby. I console myself with the idea that heartburn will be a thing of the past at least. Pillows are my only ally in all this, stacked high and plentiful. How do women with partners get on in the third trimester? There's little room left in my double bed once I arrange all the pillows around my body.

Last week the midwife had been clear about me needing to rest and I know she'll ask me again today if I've stopped working—perhaps now is the time. So far, I haven't had to use the money set aside for after the baby is born. There's been so many casual shifts at the hospital, I'd had to turn them down on occasion, and my wage has covered everything up to now. My savings and the money Colin left me in his will should see me through a period of maternity leave after the birth. It won't last as long as I'd like, but it's a relief to have it saved up ready.

My phone beeps in my pocket as I climb back into my car. Checking it, I see a message.

> **Jo:** Making stir fry for dinner tonight. Does baby still crave limes? Hope midwife went okay. See you later. X
>
> **Emma:** "Ha, baby does indeed still crave lime. Thank you. Midwife okay, talk at home. Em."

Thank goodness for Jo, I think, feeling frazzled after being nagged by a midwife for the past twenty-five minutes about my blood pressure being too high and being stressed. Realising I've been putting off replying to Lucy's message from last week, I scroll to her name:

Lucy: Hey Ems. How are you? How's Cornwall?

Emma: Sorry for the slow reply. I'm good. Cornwall is beautiful. I was on the beach this morning for a walk in the cold. How are you?

Lucy: So jealous right now that you're by the sea. Even if it is freezing. I'm the size of a beached whale, bouncing on this blooming ball, and missing you like crazy. Plus, I'm starting to forget what you look like. There's such a thing as FaceTime you know!

Emma: You know me, not a FaceTime fan—I miss you too. Still no sign of baby?

Lucy: I'm starting to think she doesn't want to meet me. I'm being induced tomorrow.

Suddenly I want to hear her voice, so I hit the call button.

"Emma!" Lucy answers on the first ring.

"Luce, I'm so excited! How are you feeling about being induced?"

"I'm scared and ready to get her out of me all at the same time."

"I can't believe she's still not made an appearance."

"Tell me about it. I'll be two weeks overdue tomorrow. I'm so uncomfortable. I've eaten hot curry, been on a walk every day, drank my fill of pineapple smoothies and tried having sex with Fynn, but who does that when they're this far along … I mean how?"

"Oh, Luce!"

"Em?"

"Yeah?"

"What if I'm a terrible mum?"

"You'll be an excellent mother. I have no doubt about that. Fynn will make an amazing father too. You're the perfect couple and this little girl is going to be so blessed to have you both as her parents. Stop worrying. When the time comes, you'll be strong, even if you can't see it yet."

"You promise?"

"I promise!"

"I've gone a bit mad buying pink things—I'm sure you can imagine."

"That doesn't sound a bit like you …"

I hear her laugh and it fills my heart with a warmth I want to keep there.

"Mum has taken up crochet. She's making a jellyfish—it's pink too."

"A pink jellyfish?" I laugh.

"I'm not entirely sure why she chose to make a jellyfish, but it's terribly cute of her."

"It really is."

"I wish you were here for all this, holding my hand as I always imagined you would be."

"I'm sorry!"

"I sound incredibly selfish because I know this trip is something you needed to do. I'm just scared that's all, excited, but petrified all at the same time."

"I'm not there in person right now, but I'm only at the end of a phone. Call me anytime."

"Have you spoken to Chris recently?"

"Not for about a month. He knows this trip is about taking some time out. Things got so intense, what with Charlotte and Andy. Colin dying and …"

"And?"

"I don't know what else I was going to say."

"You love him, though, don't you?"

"You know I do. I just can't be with him right now …"

"I do and don't get it, if I'm honest."

"How is he?"

"Sometimes he lets his guard down and I see that he's hurting a little. Missing you like crazy, trying to respect your need for time and space. Mostly I think he fights just getting in his car and hunting you down."

"Precisely why I never gave you all my address."

"You'll come back after she's born, though? I could hide it from Chris …"

"Luce, you're many things, but subtle is not one of them and you are incapable of hiding anything."

The line goes quiet.

"Lucy …"

"I'm sorry. I'm just all kinds of hormonal."

"It's okay. I get it." *More than you know.*

"I can hear Fynn's home."

"Tell him to let me know as soon as you're in labour, okay? And send him my love."

"I will."

"Speak soon."

"Love you."

"Love you."

Chapter 19

The locker room's empty and quiet as I change out of my uniform at the end of a long day triaging patients in A&E. My ankles have been swelling progressively throughout the afternoon and my back and hips are now throbbing. The midwife was right about me needing to finish working. I can barely lift my arms above my head to remove my scrub top, but I manage to wiggle out of it eventually. Replacing it with a jumper, I ease into my dark wash maternity jeans, which feel tighter than normal against my ballooning legs.

Today had been my last day at work. I'd spoken to the Lead Nurse to let her know I wasn't planning on taking anymore shifts until after my maternity leave. 'About time,' she said, smiling, before wishing me good luck and practically offering me a job once I'm back at work in a few months. It's nice being well thought of and that I have options for work when I need it in the future. Most of my shifts had been in A&E, where I felt most comfortable and I'd built up a good rapport with the staff there. I can't say that I've made anything close to a friendship, but then I'd kept myself to myself since arriving.

On my days off, I would catch up on sleep, read, or go for a long walk, usually on the beach. Jo had tried to include me in the circle of friends she'd grown up with, but I preferred the solitude. Life had become busy and complicated before leaving Pineham, so I wanted to uncomplicate things down here.

When I'd first arrived, before I was showing, one of the doctors in A&E had shown interest in me, with flirting and compliments. I was less than interested and imagined he would have got the memo sooner. However, it took him until my uniform started to fit more snugly around my midriff for him to back off. In fact, I can still see the look on his face when he found out I was pregnant.

"Night, girls," I say, leaving the changing room, feeling as though I should have mentioned it's my last shift, but not needing to make a fuss.

"Night," they chorus, smiling from behind the nurses' station.

As I walk the five-minute route back to my car, my eyelids feel heavy and my mind empty. The cool air on my warm skin, however, feels all the nicer knowing that I'm done working for the next few months. Hopefully I can relax a little in these next few weeks leading up to baby making an appearance. Not wanting to jinx anything, I've waited to buy all the baby essentials, but I'm so excited for the arrival of the cot this week. Jo bought a coming home from the hospital outfit—a pale blue and white, five-piece Winnie the Pooh set, saying she couldn't resist. I have to admit it's adorable. I've held it up so many times and thought just how tiny it is. How can I even imagine being responsible for something so small?

My phone beeps in my pocket and it's Jo, as usual. Telling me tea is almost ready. Thank goodness for her. I smile to myself and reply with a smiley face.

I pull up on the road outside our house, well, it's Jo's house, but I've come to think of it as home. All I want to do is eat and then climb into a candle-lit bath. A standard desire most evenings, particularly after work. My insides dance a little jig as I yet again savour how good it feels to have finished working for now.

"I'm back," I call out from the hallway, leaning precariously on the wall to remove my shoes from my elephant feet. "Hey," I say, entering the open plan living room/kitchen where the aroma of tomatoes and herbs warmly greets me.

"Hey you. It's lasagne for tea, if that's all right with Bubba?"

"Ha, yes, Bubba is more than all right with lasagne. Mumma, on the other hand, might regret it when she gets heartburn in the middle of the night, but then again, I get heartburn breathing in air at the moment."

She laughs.

"I would have made chicken stir fry with limes again, but it'd be the third time this week."

This time it's me who laughs.

I've loved limes since being pregnant. A wedge of lime in drinks, or squeezed on food. Even my toiletries are lime. I can't get enough of the taste, or smell. Other than fish finger sandwiches for breakfast, and plain crisps when I'd had morning sickness, lime was the only real craving I'd experienced and Jo had accommodated this so thoughtfully.

"Lasagne is perfect. I'll get my lime fix in the bubbles I'm going to add to my bath later."

"Good, well, dinner's in ten."

I go to the drawer and take out the place mats, setting them on the solid oak square dining table in the corner of the room. The house we're renting is small and cosy. Aside from this room, there are two decent-sized bedrooms and a bathroom upstairs. Jo insists it's going to be big enough for when the baby arrives, though I'm not so sure; not that I've said as much to her. There will be no escaping the noise, or mess of a baby, and I worry about disrupting Jo's life even more than I have already. Plus she's started seeing someone and it sounds as though it's getting serious. I've tried not to think about what that means for the future. All I can do is live each day in the present. Lately, though, I've been starting to wonder about going home, facing everyone and in particular Chris. The closer I get to this baby being due, the more I feel guilty for keeping this secret, for depriving him of the chance to know he's about to be a father.

Jo's lasagne hits the spot and baby is well and truly

satisfied. I offer help with the dishes, but I'm shooed away to get my bath, for which I'm grateful. As I wait for the water level to rise, I flip open the top of my lime shower gel and breathe in, my mind drifting to Chris and the numerous times I've smelt this same scent on his skin. I'm not sure if it's for this reason I'm so drawn to it, or if it's a happy coincidence. Either way, it's a sort of painful pleasure that I can't deny myself.

Naked, I stand in front of the mirror and observe my bump from the side, stroking it.

"Not long now," I whisper quietly as he stretches inside me, making me slightly lopsided. "There." I massage what feels like his bum and he moves back again. "Behave for Mummy tonight. No more two a.m. raves, please."

As I sink into the water, my eyes see a light illuminating my phone. *Chris.* I realise there's no way I'll reach it in time, sloths are probably quicker than me right now, so I let it go to voicemail.

You have one new message …

"Emma. Lucy's in labour."

I inhale.

"Everything's fine, but she wanted you to know. It all happened a little quickly in the end."

Oh, Luce.

"She wishes you were here. So do I."

Chris …

"Anyway, call me back, please. I hope you're okay? I miss hearing your voice. Bye, Em."

Chapter 20

"Hey Sis, I popped to the shop on the way up and got the magazines you asked for, plus some bottled water and chocolate supplies."

"You're a lifesaver, though I'm really tired and wonder if you'd leave me to rest?"

"But I just got here. I can read in the chair while you sleep and then if she wakes up I can hold her if you like?"

"So sweet of you, but you'll fall asleep yourself and snore and then I'll get no rest."

"Luce, are you okay?"

"I'm fine. Just tired. Stop worrying."

"Of course I'm going to worry, you're my baby sister."

"Well, as your sister, I thank you kindly for my supplies and I'm sorry to be kicking you out. Come back in a little while and you can have a cuddle with your niece."

"Deal. I'll leave you to it then. Might just pop into your loo before I go."

"No! I mean, it's for patients only."

"I won't tell if you won't."

"Seriously, Chris. There's a visitors' toilet on the way out."

"Okay, okay. Call off the toilet police. Love you. Sleep tight."

I push open the bathroom door and step into the room, but don't speak.

"He's gone. So, now do you want to tell me what's going on?"

"I'm sorry." Tears huddle together in my eyes, making them blurry.

"Is it Chris's?"

"Yes. Thank you for not giving me away just now."

Lucy's holding her chest, her eyes searching the bedsheet covering her legs. "He deserves to know the truth … Emma, how could you keep this from us? I deserved to know," she almost shouts, but lowers her tone when the baby stirs.

"I'm sorry," I repeat. "I almost fell apart just now hearing his voice from inside the bathroom. I didn't want to lie to you, any of you."

"So why did you?" Finally, she makes eye contact with me.

"There are too many reasons, but mainly because I just didn't want it to happen again."

"What?"

"For someone else to be with me because I'm having their baby, Luce. You saw what happened with Matt."

"Chris isn't Matt, Emma. In fact, he couldn't be more different."

"I know he isn't, but I'm still me and I just panicked. Finally, I had everything I wanted, including this baby, and I was going to tell him, of course I was. Then he started talking as though he didn't want kids, which completely threw me. Then I started thinking about last time, how I was just starting to get excited about all of it when I miscarried, and my thoughts ran away with me. My heart felt too fragile to deal with any of it, so I chose to go away to Cornwall with Jo for a while. I begin to sob.

"Come here," she says, her mood softening as she holds out her arms and I sink into them. "Emma, why didn't you talk to me about any of this?"

"Because you're his sister, Luce, and I didn't want to put you in that position. It was the first time that I couldn't even confide in you. I've missed you. I've missed you so much."

"I've missed you too," she replies, neither of us able to fight back tears.

I sit back and place my hand on the cot beside her bed. "Hello you, I'm your Aunty Emma … I hope?"

"You don't need to ask me that."

Smiling, I carry on staring at my niece. "Can I hold her?"

"Of course."

As I cradle her, a wave of excitement courses through me. "She's absolutely beautiful, Luce."

She sighs. "Thank you. I think so too. Though her

entrance into the world was a little more stressful than I'd have liked."

"I know. I'm just pleased that you're both healthy and safe. Have you decided on a name?"

"Amelia Rose."

"I love it."

"Hello, Amelia Rose." I slide my fingertip gently down her soft cheek. "I could actually eat her, she's so delicious!"

"Please don't."

We both laugh.

"How many weeks are you?"

"Thirty-four, and it's a boy."

I watch as tears, once again, flow down her cheeks.

"I'm making you sad. Perhaps I shouldn't have come?"

"I'm not sad, I'm so relieved and happy to see you. It's just such a lot to take in at once. I do want you here." Her voice sounds choked with all the emotion.

"Even after lying and abandoning you?"

"Seeing how destroyed you were when you got divorced and remembering how hard losing the baby was for you. I get it. I won't pretend to like it, and you didn't need to run, but I get why you did. Your head must have been spinning."

I feel more relief hearing her words than I've felt for months. I'm home and with Lucy, which is where I want to be.

"So many times I just wanted to hear your voice and tell you everything, I felt as if I'd backed myself into a corner."

"Well, you're here now and I'm not letting you go again."

"I can live with that."

"How's the pregnancy been?" Lucy asks.

"Morning sickness was tough, otherwise I've been okay. I'm tired now it's getting towards the end."

"You will be, but it's worth it."

Our conversation is culled by the sound of the door creaking open behind me.

"Emma?"

Turning slowly, I can hear my heartbeat echoing in my ears.

"Hi, Fynn," I say, to my relief.

"Well, that explains a few things," he says before coming over to hug me around my bump and his daughter in my arms. I pass her to Fynn and sit down.

"How are you doing?" he asks Lucy, sitting beside her, leaving a kiss on her forehead.

"I'm fine." She strokes his arm.

"I assume Chris doesn't know?" His eyes are cold.

"No." I watch his face say everything his mouth isn't. "Just say it, Fynn."

He looks me in the eye, his skin a tinge of red. "He'd want to know if you're carrying his child, Em."

"I know I've upset people keeping this a secret. I had my reasons, though, Fynn," I say, standing up. "I'm going to get going. Today isn't about me."

"Please don't leave." Lucy moves quickly and grabs my hand.

I smile at her. "I'll be back, I promise. I've excited

you enough for one day." I lift her hand to my mouth and kiss it.

By the time I pull up in the car park of the estate, I'm having second thoughts about facing him. I felt quite confident on the drive here from the hospital, resolute even. Now, though, I feel as though my stomach is churning acid as I walk towards the door. I lift my hand as I reach it, but it rests mid-air. I take a deep breath and knock, nibbling at the loose piece of skin on my dry bottom lip while I wait.

"Emma?"

"Hi, Sylvia." I greet the housekeeper.

"Well, don't you look absolutely radiant," she says, holding open the door for me.

"Thank you. I'm not sure radiant is how I feel."

"Are you here for Christopher, darling?"

"Yes, I've just seen Lucy at the hospital, so I'm here to see Chris. If he's in?"

"How's she doing? And the baby?"

"She's fine and the baby's gorgeous!"

"We're all so looking forward to meeting the little one."

I smile.

"Christopher's in his office. I'll phone him to tell him you're here, save your legs."

"No, thank you. I'll go to him."

"I'll get knitting. Do you know what you're having?"

"It's a boy."

"How wonderful."

I smile at her excitement, but know she must be wondering who the father is. All will be revealed soon enough, I think as I make my way to his office.

The door's open, so I step inside clutching at my coat in front of me. I hear the jangle of a collar and see Barney rushing towards me. He seems to know not to jump up onto me, somehow, as I stoop to stroke him. Though it doesn't stop him whipping my leg excitedly with his tail, and trailing me to Chris's desk. I'm flushed now from walking and the change in temperature from the outside to in here. As I reach his desk, I close my eyes and imagine him sitting behind it, wearing his blue polo shirt, smiling at me. When I open them, I notice something on his desk—a book I gave to him for his twenty-first birthday. When I pick it up, a Polaroid photograph drops out. It's of Chris and me, taken years ago. We'd been messing around, posing with our tongues sticking out, being daft together. I'd seen the other photos we'd taken that day, but never this one. I'm smiling into the camera and Chris is looking at me with the same look in his eye he had the first night we made love.

"Emma."

I stiffen, closing my eyes. I hadn't heard anyone come into the room. Taking a steady breath, I slowly turn to face him, lowering my coat and his gaze lands on my swollen belly. He does a double take and shuffles back a step.

"Chris …" I stammer, my breath hitched. There are no words that will make this situation right in his eyes.

"Is it mine?"

I let go of my breath. "Of course it's yours, how can you ask me that?"

"Oh, I dunno, maybe because you've kept this a secret from me?" He gestures one hand in the air, then runs his open palm down his face, resting it into a fist over his mouth.

"Jo drove me home after I listened to your voicemail about Lucy being in labour."

"So, Lucy knows?"

"Only today, I promise."

"That's why Lucy was acting so strange?"

"I was in the bathroom."

He's shaking his head. "Emma, I'm … I'm struggling to get my head around this. I mean I'm dreaming, right? This has got to be a dream, because my best friend of my entire life and the woman that I've loved for years, wouldn't leave and hide that she's pregnant with my child?" His gaze is unfixed, moving from place to place.

"I was scared."

"What of? That I'd be a lousy father to this baby?"

"I would never think that."

"What then? Did you not want to be with me?"

"Of course I wanted to be with you—I was terrified of losing the baby, of what that might do to you, to us. We finally got on track, after all these years and all our sagas. I didn't want this to be how we started our relationship, Chris. And I didn't want to end up with someone who was doing the right thing by me again. I didn't want you by default!"

"Want me by default? What do you mean want me by default?"

"You said yourself just days before I left that you didn't want children. I knew I was pregnant and I was about to tell you."

"I never said I didn't want children."

"You said all that stuff about being able to give them back and Fynn taking the news about becoming a dad better than you would."

"A few comments and that's it, I don't deserve to know all this time that I'm going to be a father. All this time, Emma! I mean, why now? You may as well live the lie a little longer! Why not just let the kid find me when they're eighteen!"

"Chris, I ..."

"Or is it Andy's? Were you not sure who the father was?"

"You know I never slept with him."

"That's what you told me, Em, but maybe you hid that detail from me too."

"Okay. I get you're angry and that's fine. I just came here to tell you the truth and now you know." As I walk past him, he doesn't even look at me. Barney tries to follow, but I whisper, "Stay." My eyes are stinging with hot tears, being held back only by my pride and desire not to make a scene.

Pushing back the door to my parents' house, I step inside the kitchen to see Mum at the table on her laptop.

"Darling." She leaps to her feet and rushes over to me. "You've bloomed since I last saw you. How are you? Come, sit."

I ease into a chair in the lounge, Mum didn't even suggest the kitchen table to sit at, which is just as well, given how achy I feel tonight.

"I'm just tired, Mum. Turns out it's a long way home from Cornwall."

The rise of her left eyebrow tells me she's fully aware how far away I've been all this time and how unimpressed she still is. Not that she's said as much.

"I'm sorry, Mum. For going away and keeping all those secrets … for asking you to keep my secrets."

"Thank you for the apology. I won't say you haven't disappointed me, Emma, but I do know just how hard last year was for you, and I've never lost a baby before, so I can't truly understand the pain and confusion it leaves behind. All I wish is that you had come to me when you found out you were pregnant, instead of going away suddenly, leaving us all wondering what on earth happened. I could have talked things through with you, made you feel able to face it, and Chris."

"He knows, by the way!"

"When?"

"I almost saw him at the hospital—I hid in the bathroom, actually. Then after speaking to Lucy I felt ready to face him, so I went straight to the estate."

"And, how did he take the news?"

"About as well as you'd imagine he'd take the news that I'm eight months pregnant with the baby he knows nothing about."

"Well, it has to be a shock, love. I mean, give him some time to process and I'm sure he'll come round and talk."

"Of course, he's allowed to be shocked and angry, and not come round to the idea at all if he doesn't want to. I chose this, he didn't, so I don't expect anything from him."

"He won't leave you to have this baby alone."

"I'm not scared of having this baby alone. I want to be a mum. I've wanted it for a very long time now. I'm happy. The kind of happy that only comes from yourself and knowing what you want from life. I miss him, of course I do. I wish I'd acted differently back then, but I don't regret this baby one bit."

She stands up, leaning over to hug me.

"I'm proud of you, Emma. For doing the right thing and for finding your own happiness. I love you and this little bundle, so very much."

"We love you too, Mum."

Perching on the edge of my bed, I breathe in the comforting smell of home. I stare at the plate of sandwiches and glass of milk Mum brought me upstairs, not feeling much like a big meal tonight. My mind is empty, as though every last one of my thoughts and emotions have been exhumed. Yet, I feel surprisingly at peace, with a sense of calm I've been lacking for a long time. I may have found my inner happiness in Cornwall these past few months, but I never found inner peace. Now though, it's there, deep seated at my core. Chris is upset, yes, but he knows the truth, as does Lucy. No more secrets and lies. Whatever happens from here on in will at least be the truth, plain and simple.

There's a knock on the door and it opens before I have chance to answer.

"Can I come in?" Chris is standing in the doorway, his features soft and tinged with sadness.

"Of course."

"Your mum said to come up."

"Are you okay?"

"Honestly, I'm not sure. I'm sorry for getting so angry with you, though."

"It was deserved. I know I have a lot of explaining to do."

"Em, I just want to understand it. I'm struggling with why you couldn't tell me about this. We were finally in a good place, with no complications and drama."

"Exactly, no complications for what seemed liked the first time in forever … Matt and I started this way, remember. Happy and in love one day, pregnant the next and then life imploded. My whole married life with Matt I never knew, wholeheartedly, that he would have been with me if I hadn't fallen pregnant. This time around, I wanted no doubt in my mind that the man I want to spend the rest of my life with is with me because he chooses to be, not because he feels obliged to be. Plus, you told me that you didn't want kids, so I had to get away."

"Emma, you don't get it, do you? There's not a day that goes by where I don't think that if I hadn't lost myself and my mind all those years ago, we could have been together all this time and how much heartache I could have saved you. How I'd imagined we might have a child or two by now …" He reaches out slowly, touching my bump. "I know you think I said I didn't want kids, but that's not true. I couldn't bear the idea of loving a child and losing them, or anything bad happening to them."

"Chris." Tears burn my cheeks as they fall.

"The truth, Emma Millar, is I love you and I want lots of babies with you. The more the better as far as I'm concerned. Fear's held us both back for too long in this life."

I laugh, wiping my splotchy, tear-soaked cheeks with the back of my hand as he passes me a tissue.

"You're very well prepared, Mr Golding."

"You have me well trained, Miss Millar." He pulls me into his arms, our lips meeting, and it's as if the past seven months have fallen away.

"Fancy a walk?" I ask him.

"Aren't you tired?"

"I'm always tired, but I'm restless at this time of night."

"We can go for a walk. Maybe back at the estate, take Barney out too." He pauses to look at me. "Emma."

"My coat slides to the floor as I grip my lower back with my hand.

"Emma! Are you all right?" he says, placing his hand on my hunched back.

"I've got pain in my back. It's not right. Chris, something's not right."

Chapter 21

Chris abandons his car in a pick-up only zone, but I'm in too much pain to care. It's not long before I'm in a wheelchair being pushed along at speed, by Chris. I hear him talking to someone on the intercom and then a buzz sound rings out as the doors slide open.

"Hello, Emma, I'm one of the midwives who'll be assessing you. Who's this you have with you?" She's asking me as she takes over pushing the chair, also at speed.

"This is the baby's father, Chris," I utter and can't help but feel how strange those words sound and yet, somehow, just as I've always wanted them to.

"So you have pain in your lower back?"

"Yes. All of a sudden—really intense pain," I say in a strained voice.

"Have you hurt yourself, fallen, been in any kind of accident?"

"No."

"And how's the pregnancy been?" she asks, stopping in a room, offering me a hand to get onto the trolley.

"My blood pressure's been high, otherwise okay. I

think I'm bleeding too." I lower my head, knowing this is going to worry Chris even more. I didn't mention to him that I thought I was bleeding. When he'd asked me in the car if I was okay, I'd told him that I was; other than that, we were silent.

"Is everything all right?" he asks the midwife, clearing his throat. His fingertips are in danger of rubbing away the skin on his temple.

"Let's have a look at both mum and baby and see what's happening, shall we?" She gives Chris a reassuring smile that wavers.

A sudden weakness takes hold of me and I feel light-headed. I cry out in pain as I slip down the bed, my limbs heavy. A warm hand grasps mine as I hear ringing and a faint sound of my name being called. It's cold in here. The room sounds fuller, but all I can see is bright lights and a wash of blurry faces. Some look as though they're talking to me, I see their lips moving, but hear no sound other than the ringing. A burst of air tickles my lips, accompanied by the smell of plastic. My arm's being held by someone who's tapping the back of my hand. I feel a sting, followed by a trickle of coolness rushing upwards, beneath my skin. There's a clunking sound either side of me, jolting me. I'm floating now, the ceiling moving above me. Voices are fading further away as the wind around me picks up speed. I cry out one final time as everything goes black.

There he is, waiting in a windowless room no bigger than the width of his arm span. Sitting on a green chair, staring at the white walls that are the same colour as his complexion. He doesn't sit long, before pacing the room. I see him, but I have this odd feeling that I'm dreaming.

"Why is it taking so long?"

I hear him.

It's so real this dream. Where are we?

"Cath!"

Mum and Dad are here.

"Christopher, what happened?" *she asks.*

"She just collapsed after we got here … the baby's heart rate dropped and they rushed her to theatre."

The baby?

Mum's shoulders sink and I see Dad guide her to a chair as Chris takes her hand.

Time passes and I'm stuck watching my loved ones. Chris is sitting with his head bowed, resting his elbows on his knees.

I want to hold him so badly.

"I'm sorry you had to find out like this, Christopher. I wanted her to tell you." *She touches his back.*

"You knew I was the father?"

"Not at first, but eventually and for some time now."

His eyes narrow—he's disappointed in her.

"I don't blame you for not telling me. I just want her to be okay. Why is it taking so long?"

There's a man, dressed in scrubs walking towards them and they all rise to their feet in an instant.

"Who's the next of kin?" *the doctor asks.*

"We're her parents and this is the baby's father."

"Please, take a seat," *he says, gesturing towards the nearby chairs, his expression unreadable.*

Dad's holding Mum's hand as she takes Chris's arm, gripping it.

"Firstly, mother and baby are both fine."

I hear a collective sigh reverberate around the room.

"It was touch and go in theatre for a time and we lost Emma briefly, before stabilising the bleeding. She's in theatre recovery now and as soon as she's stable, we'll transfer her to obstetrics high dependency unit for monitoring."

"High dependency?"

"Emma suffered something called placental abruption, probably from underlying pre-eclampsia. We're replacing her blood loss with blood transfusions. We just need to keep a close eye on her for now."

"Is she awake?" *Chris asks, but I know the answer.*

"Not yet."

I'm no longer in the waiting room. Instead, opposite a long desk, there are four beds and I'm standing at the foot of one of them. I look peaceful sleeping, aside from the oxygen tubing in my nose and a bag of blood attached to the needle in my hand. I feel as if I'm at work, staring at the monitor of a patient and charting down their observations. Except they're my observations and it's me in the bed.

Then I hear something, a faint murmur beside me. I peer

down into the cot and see him, my son. Tears build in my eyes as I'm taken aback by how perfect he is, how small, how precious. How loved he is already. I want to memorise this moment and cherish it forever.

Wake up, I tell myself. Wake up so you can hold your beautiful baby boy.

The door opens and I hear Mum and Chris.

"You can hold him if you like?" *I hear an unfamiliar voice say before seeing Chris lean over the cot.*

"He looks so peaceful. I wish she could see him," *says Chris.*

I can.

"She will soon." *Mum rubs Chris's back as he lifts up our baby … Our baby.* "He's perfect, Christopher. Just perfect." *Her smile and tone reflects every inch of the pride she feels. Turning to me, I watch Mum stroke my cheek and feel the tingle of her smooth, light touch on my skin—an odd sensation given how removed I currently am from my body.* "You'll know this soon enough, but as a parent you would rather change places with your child than watch them injured or ill."

"I think I can feel some of that already."

She begins to cry.

"Your daughter is the strongest woman I know."

Be strong and wake up.

It feels as though it's early in the morning as I look down at Chris, asleep, head down on the bed, holding my hand. My nose itches so I move my hand to scratch it, causing him to jolt awake.

"Hey, it's okay. I'm here." He leans in closer.

"You're here …" I cough, suddenly aware of how much every part of my body aches.

"Where else would I be?"

I'm here, I realise.

"Where's Mum?" I say, weakly, my mind desperately trying to piece together what's going on and if what I saw really happened?

"She's outside. I'll tell the midwife you're awake."

"No." I go to grab his hand as he stands, but my weary arm flops beside me. Pausing, he rests his hand over mine where it now lies. "I just want to see him." My gaze drifts to the cot beside my bed. His fingertips trace my skin as he removes his hand before lifting him out.

"Here's your mummy, little man. I'd told you she'd be awake soon." As he lowers him down for me, I can see him clearly for the first time. His head's covered with a small, white knitted hat that rests loosely on it and there are tiny creases either side of his forehead, above tufts of light brown hair all wispy around his ears. His eyes are puffy and firmly closed, his arms turned upwards and in, towards his ears—like he doesn't have a care in the world.

My heart bubbles with warmth, and a tear rolls down my cheek as I lift my hand to stroke his face.

"He's so perfect."

"Just like his mum," Chris says.

"Can I hold him, please?"

He places him in my arms, leaving his hand there for support. I must look as weak as I feel. I gaze down at my son, whose head is moving in tiny circles as if to tell me he's been disturbed by us picking him up.

"Hey baby boy, it's your mummy. Sorry I wasn't there straight away, but I'm not going anywhere ever again, I promise." Kissing his head, my nose loitering on his skin, I breathe in a more intoxicating smell than I've ever known. As I let go of my breath, Chris senses I'm tired, so he lifts him back up and into his cot.

"You're awake." The midwife appears. "How are you feeling, Emma?"

"Sore, weak—but happy."

"You have a beautiful little boy. Have you held him?"

"Just," Chris answers. "But she was getting tired."

I move my head so slowly I'm not sure it even constitutes nodding.

"You'll be quite fatigued for a while, Emma. Rest while you can. I'll fetch you something for the pain."

"Thank you." I then turn to Chris. "I'm thirsty, can I have a sip of water, please?"

"Of course." He fills my glass and holds it so the straw rests on my lips. After a sip, I let my head flop back onto the pillow.

"I'll get your parents."

"Wait. How's Luce?"

"She's fine. Baby's fine and they're both at home. She wanted to be here, but Fynn's told her to wait until you're awake."

I smile. "Good. Jo, I need to call Jo, she'll be so worried."

"I've spoken to her. I had your phone when she rang."

"She's been amazing these past few months."

His brows pull together. "I could have been amazing, if you'd let me."

"Chris …"

"You've had us so worried." Mum rushes beside me, giving me a lingering hug.

"I'm sorry, Mum."

She strokes my face with the back of her hand and I feel a sense of déjà vu.

"Do you like your grandson, Dad?" I ask my father, who's standing over his cot, staring down at him.

"He's a strapping lad. I think he'll make a great farmer," he says, smiling, as we all laugh. "Anyway, come on, love, they told us we could only stay for a minute." He turns to me. "I think I need to get your mother home for a sleep, she's exhausted." He kisses my cheek. "Well done, darlin'. You get some rest, too, ya hear."

"I'll try. Love you, Dad."

"I don't like leaving you." I kiss Mum as she leans over me to say a reluctant goodbye.

"I'm okay, get some sleep. You'll need it." I nod in the direction of the cot.

"Call me if you need me. I'll be straight back at visiting time. I love you."

"Love you, Mum."

Chris has picked up our son and Mum creeps over to them. "See you later, my gorgeous grandson." She kisses his head, before hugging Chris loosely around his shoulders.

We're alone now, the three of us. Chris sitting beside me, rocking him in his strong, safe arms. "I'm a little bit addicted to holding him. Though I'm not sure we'll be saying that in a few weeks when he's crying every time we try and put him down."

I cry, my eyes sore from what feels like months of tears.

"Hey, don't cry. It's a happy day."

"These aren't sad tears. It's just you said 'we'! I've missed you so much, Chris. It's been so hard doing this without you. I wanted to tell you every day. What you said about a reality where we'd been together and had children, it broke me. You, me and this baby—it's my dream."

"Hey," he says, sitting on the bed, resting his forehead against mine. "I'm here now, we have a beautiful son to cherish, and I'm not going anywhere. I can promise you that."

I breathe in his words as though I'm dreaming.

"There is one thing that isn't quite right about all this."

"Oh," I say and bite my lip.

"He needs a name."

"Phew." My lips part. "I wondered what you were going to say. I've had a little while to think about this and, well … how would you would feel about calling him Stephen?"

He halts, his hands gripping the sides of the cot as he stares down at our sleeping baby.

"I'm sorry, I don't want to upset you."

"I'm not upset. It's perfect, Em." He runs his hand across the blanket covering him. "Stephen … Your uncle would have loved you."

"He would have been an amazing uncle," I agree.

"The best," he replies, perching beside me on the bed, holding my hand. Our fingertips entwine, circling in and out as if it's the most natural thing in the world, and it is. Together, complete.

"Can I ask you something?"

He nods.

"How long have you loved me?"

He lifts his hand, tracing the outline of my face. "Forever. Just sorry I left it so long to tell you."

"Better late than never," I say, heat radiating through my chest.

"Timing's everything," he whispers, drawing closer.

"I love you, Chris." Is all I say as he leans down to kiss me.

Epilogue

Then I hear something, a faint murmur beside me. I peer down into the cot and see him, my son. Tears build in my eyes as I'm taken aback by how perfect he is, how small, how precious. How loved he is already. I want to memorise this moment and cherish it forever.

Wake up, I tell myself. Wake up so you can hold your beautiful baby boy.

I'm upright, checking the cot beside us as Chris leans over.

"You okay?"

"I had that dream again. The one where I'm standing over his cot in the hospital, while my body's in the bed." I slow my breathing and he rubs my shoulders, lightly kissing my neck.

"Hey, it's okay, you're fine. We're all here together. Now, get dressed, I have a surprise for you."

Last night was the May Ball and so this morning we're joined for breakfast by my parents, Lucy, Fynn, baby Amelia, Jo—who used the ball as an excuse to visit, Chris's parents, and of course, Granny.

Baby Stephen is a typical boy, feeding all night and sleepy in the day, though my tiredness fades into the background as I look to my left, pulling in a deep breath as I see him with his grandmas, my mum holding him in her arms as Elizabeth entertains him with a toy giraffe. Lucy is standing with Fynn to my right, smiling down at their daughter who's in Granny's stiff and unsure arms.

"I think Amelia needs a change." Granny wrinkles up her nose, turning her head sideways and holding her up at arm's length, as though she were Rafiki from *The Lion King*.

"Do you want to change her, Gran?" Lucy asks, rolling her lips together, trying to stifle a smirk, though failing miserably.

"Oh no, dear, we didn't change nappies in my day. We had a nanny for that sort of thing … here." There's a rumble of laughter that she ignores, slipping to the back of the room as the aroma of something a little less pleasant fills the air. Despite her offhand ways, she's part of the uniqueness of this family—*our family*, and you can't help but love her in spite of it all.

I feel the most content I have in a very long time, with all the people I care about most in life under one roof. Jo has somehow managed to steal Stephen from Mum and as our eyes meet across the room, I smile at her with unspoken gratitude. I will never be able to repay her for all she's done for me.

Lucy is on the floor changing Amelia, as an attentive Fynn passes her a clean nappy and it strikes me how picture perfect the scene in front of me is. Except for Chris, who I now notice is missing.

The door opens and the housekeeper enters the room. "Mr Christopher asked me to give you this." She hands me a folded piece of paper.

"Thank you, Sylvia," I say.

As I unfold the note, the words make my heart slow to a rhythm reserved only for him.

Emma,

Leave Stephen with his adoring grandparents.

Meet me in the treehouse.

C x

I walk the route through to the treehouse that is now as familiar to me as when we'd been children. It's not as warm as last May, but the sun is shining down on me, adding to my happy mood. The past year has taught me that I am braver, I am stronger and I hope I'm smarter from everything that's happened. There was no way I could have known this time last year what pain and joy awaited me, nor would I have been able to predict how it would end.

The air begins to fill with a familiar piece of music drifting towards me. It's coming from the treehouse, which doesn't make me think about any of the sad times the treehouse has borne witness to. Rather, I think about how all these events brought Chris and I closer together over the years.

Illuminated in a patch of sun filtering through the treeline, the red and white roses Colin planted look as beautiful in full bloom, shielding the treehouse, as he intended them to. Beneath is a memory bench with the words: 'In loving memory of Colin and Rose, his favourite Rose of them all' carved into the wood.

The music I can hear is louder now, as Chris appears and climbs down the ladder to meet me, carrying two roses, one white, and one red. He pulls my waist towards him and kisses me lightly, making the hairs on my neck stand on end.

"Tchaikovsky?" I say, one eyebrow raised.

"It's your favourite." He begins swaying me in time with the music.

"You remembered?" I tilt my head, pausing.

"I remember the list you made." He lifts his arm for me to spin under it.

"Didn't you always tease me about my list?" I say, pressing my lips into a fine line.

"A boy always teases the girl he's in love with."

"Is that right?" I say, wrinkling my nose and he kisses me again. The sun warms our bodies as I nuzzle into his chest. When the music quickens, he spins me faster and I let the carefree, happy rhythm absorb me.

I tilt back my head until I feel dizzy and together we laugh. When the tempo slows again he pulls me close, resting his nose on mine. I swallow, closing my eyes. When I open them, he's pulling me by the hand towards the foot of the ladder.

"Climb up!"

Placing my feet carefully, I climb as the music reaches its crescendo. When I arrive at the top of the ladder, it falls silent. Fairy lights line the roof and back wall of the treehouse. The floor is scattered with cushions, blankets and red and white rose petals. My heart drums against my chest as I turn back to Chris, who is down on one knee.

"*You and me forever*—that's what you made me promise, right here in this very treehouse, all those year ago. He opens a delicate black box to reveal a single solitaire diamond ring, taking my left hand in his. "I'm madly in love with you, Emma Millar and I'm madly in love with our son. Would his mum do me the honour of becoming my wife?"

"Yes … yes … yes." Happy tears blur my vision as he slips the ring onto my finger. I fall into his arms and right then my world is more complete than I'd ever imagined possible. This was the ending that I never saw coming and the one I wanted most of all. In this moment, I realise that perhaps, some histories are worth repeating, with the right person.

The End

Acknowledgements

I started writing *Meet Me in the Treehouse*, in 2014 after my marriage ended. At first, it was a form of therapy—cheaper than actual therapy. However, it wasn't long before I realised how much I enjoy writing. Emma starts out in a similar place to where I was and her emotional journey reflects my own. I loved creating her world; her childhood home on the farm, in the village where she grew up. Her safe place, with family and friends who love her. The magic of creating places and people as I did in this story, warmed even my own heart at a time when I needed all the warmth I could get. Chris came along when I needed a hero in my life. It didn't matter he was just fantasy; a creation far from my own experiences. I wrote him to be everything I wanted in someone, flaws and all. Perhaps all writers have a work of fiction that's personal. Maybe all works of fiction are, to some extent. *Meet Me in the Treehouse*, will always be special to me and I hope you've enjoyed Emma and Chris's journey. Thank you for your support. This means everything to me.

I want to thank Hilary Johnson's Author Advisory Service for that first critique of my book in 2016, which forced me to rewrite and produce a far stronger story. More recently, Hilary's editorial services helped me to get it in shape for publishing. Thank you to the Romantic Novelists' Association New Writers' Scheme members and organisers for the manuscript critique, the wonderful people I've met, and the things I've learnt since joining this year. Thanks in particular to Janet Gover for all your help and encouragement. Thank you to the lovely Heidi Swain for her never-ending advice; she has been both a source of knowledge and encouragement in my writing since 2016, when I first messaged her for some author advice. Huge thanks to Nicola May for the self-publishing tips, which have been invaluable in achieving my dream of publication.

To Emma-Claire Wilson and Isabella May and my twitter writing friends, thank you for your advice and support. I would also like to say thank you to the late Andrew Wright for his guidance, Philip Cumberland for your self-publishing tips, Elaine Coulborn for your midwife knowledge and helping me understand my character's journey and my cousin Jayne for her editing in the beginning where all the characters drank tea far too much. What can I say, I grew up in Derbyshire.

Thank you to my awesome parents for buying me the laptop I used to write this book. It was a thirtieth birthday present and I think it's been worth the investment. You are both my rocks and I'm privileged to call you, first, my Mum and Dad and, second, my best friends. I remember when Dad gave me a shop catalogue for Christmas, covered with A4 paper that had the title of my novel and my pen name on it. Your belief in me knows no bounds.

To my Beta reader RJ, my Sister from another mister, original Beta reader and the only person who has read my chapters almost as many times as I have. You are constant in my life and have never given up on me or tired of listening to me. Thank you for truly believing in this dream of mine and knowing I'd succeed. We did it!

Thank you Beth and Lauren; Smemories book club and besties. I love that my novel inspired our book club name and I always smile when I reach that part of the story. You bring me joy and laughter, ladies. You've listened and advised and listened and advised. When I didn't want to carry on, you told me I could do it. Thanks to both of you, and Beth for Beta reading my novel. No one will ever reach your reading speeds, or possess as little will power to not read ahead in book club (Tom, you must find better hiding places for your wife's books).

Mother-in-law (MIL) and Father-in-law (FIL) Joan and Les, thank you for your faith in me. I love that while my MIL was engrossed in my story, my FIL kept her supplied with tea and snacks. You are both wonderfully supportive.

My girlies: Jo Dude, Ali, Manni, Ellie and Lianne. You listened to me waffle on about this book for what must feel like a decade, though it isn't … quite. You've been my sounding board, my pep talks and my inspirations. I remember when Manni first read some chapters and was late home, having completely forgotten the time. I knew then that I had something.

Kate, there are no words to express how much your friendship means to me, I will always treasure you. Xania, thank you for inspiring me and for being the friend who lifted me through my darkness.

To all my office buddies new and old who have heard me talk about this book so often—the highs, the lows and everything in between—thank you.

My late grandparents were so much inspiration—especially my grandpa for always smelling like pigs and naming them after me. I miss you all and wish you could read this book.

I've saved the very best until last. James, my favourite human and person to edit books with. You are, without doubt, the sweetest, most generous man I know. You and the boys are my entire world. Thank you for being the reason I keep going each and every day. I love you all.

About the Author

Kelly Tink is a cancer nurse, writer and hopeless romantic, living in Cambridgeshire. She enjoys exploring fun outdoor places with her husband and two sons, especially if it involves eating ice cream by the sea.

She's an avid reader, loves a good film or TV series and drinks lots of tea. *Meet Me in the Treehouse* is Kelly's debut novel. She can be found tweeting at @kelly_tink.

It would mean the world to Kelly if you would consider taking a few moments to write a review. These reviews let new readers know what you thought of *Meet Me in the Treehouse.* Thank you.

Website: kellytink.com

Copyright

First Published in Great Britain by Middlemist Publishing 2020

Print Edition

Cover design and illustration by Mark Standbrook. tall2d.com

A catalogue copy of this book is available from the British Library.

ISBN: 978-1-5272-6982-8

Printed in Great Britain
by Amazon

56787604R00161